To Joe
Best we
Please forg
Stephen has corrected them
since!

Imelda xx

THE LAST EXIT

Imelda Megannety

THE LAST EXIT

By the same author

Song without words
Kaleidoscope
Her Sixth Sense
Return to Moineir

Cover from oil painting by Marie-Claire Keague

www.marieclairekeague.com

Prologue

Charlie put his arm round his mother's shoulders. She was shaken by sobs which she tried to stifle at times, for the boys' sake.

The church seemed so empty. Judy thought about all her mother's friends who should have been here to see Vera off on her final journey. The text messages and emails were too numerous to reply to just now. The priest was speaking quietly but Judy heard nothing. The few people in the church felt so distant and alone. Not being able to even shake hands or hug the bereaved relatives in their grief, was somehow sadder and felt so inhuman.

A couple of Judy's work mates attended, and some old friends of Vera, just ten in all, that was all that was allowed, in this present time of lockdown.

Why had Judy not listened to her mother? She was not demented after all. She had warned her daughter of the danger she was in and Judy had not listened. She was convinced that Vera wanted to return to their home and was trying to frighten Judy into finishing her relationship with Tommy.

Well, her mother had been right all along. When Judy thought of the three months before Covid 19 broke on the world, she knew that she was in deep trouble in her private life and that her boys were also at risk. But then, that big C came; visitors were not allowed to visit the retirement home. A telephone conversation would have been too painful, so it was always a rushed call or card sent in the post to say she would visit as soon as possible.

Then the virus had struck Rosebank, both the staff and the residents. One of the staff, although sick, had worked two shifts and after that, many people fell sick.

Now it was too late to say, 'Sorry Mum, you were right to be worried.' She knew that her mother would be relieved to know that her house was peaceful again; the threat of violence and actual abuse was gone; Tommy was gone, and this time was given a realistic prison sentence. His former wife was also happy to know about this.

Was there a life after domestic abuse? Judy did not know. She had her job to keep her busy, mentally and physically. She hoped her boys would recover and not suffer any effects from witnessing Tommy's behaviour.

She wondered now, how she could have been so misled; Tommy was charming, so attentive and helpful, so skilled in the kitchen and seemingly interested in the boys and their lives.

Time went by, and her friends had become absent, she realised that she was all alone with Tommy. He did not approve of her friends; he wanted her all to himself, he explained. At first this flattered her and made her feel very important to him, but as time passed, there was a loneliness in her life, her friends avoided her and now it seemed that Tommy did not want her to visit or receive any visitors and what was worse, she had to give an account now, of all her movements in her day.

If they visited a restaurant or pub, he started accusing her of looking at other men. When it began, she burst out laughing, but then seeing his tight and angry face she remonstrated. However, once it started, it kept accelerating. Now it was the boys who were on edge and being stifled. When they were gradually being worn down and threatened with curses and vague sinister warnings, that was when she knew there was something terribly wrong with Tommy.

It took a couple of beatings before she decided enough was enough. She was frightened that he would harm the boys and that was when she went to the police.

She had been so relieved to find a sympathetic ear there. The woman she dealt with; Marie Duffy was so understanding. Later she learned that the woman had been expecting her from something her mother had said to a colleague of hers. Judy could not believe it. Because of her mother's chance remark to a sergeant at the retirement home, she felt that these people already knew her, and she felt much better after reporting her abuse. They believed her, and that boosted her self-confidence which had been so eroded. Now the healing could begin and her relationship with her boys could mend and start again.

Chapter 1

Judy drove up the long drive to Rosebank House slowly. Her mother beside her, looked out at the landscaped gardens glimpsed behind the tree-lined avenue. It was then it really sank in. This is it, Vera thought, my new and probable last home. When it had been discussed over the past six months it had not seemed real. Going into a retirement home or old-aged home, as she thought of it, was for old people who lived alone and could not cope. She had felt years away from that scenario then and hoped it would never happen. She knew that Judy was struggling and at times seemed at her wits end. She was not the cause of such stress, surely? It was those unruly pre-teenage boys that had Judy so stressed.

Her daughter was her only child and as Vera herself, had been a bit of a tearaway as a teenager, so Vera understood completely. But then she had a father in her life; Judy's husband had found being a parent of three energetic and unpredictable boys too much and had decided to take a job that brought him to a different country. Now his visits were so infrequent and traumatic, and his wife felt they had drifted so far apart that they were as good as separated.

Vera sighed and wished that Judy had chosen a better man. Poor Michael was an only son and totally spoiled rotten by his doting mother.

Judy, misinterpreting the long sigh she heard, slowed the car.

'Mum, you know that you are only staying here for a short period of time. It's just that I need breathing space to cope with Alan and Joe. Charlie is starting boarding school in September and that will be a big help to me, you know?'

'Yes, I understand that darling. You must get your life together now and not rely on Michael anymore. You need to get professional help with the twins, I think. They are too friendly with the wrong sort of young fellows and you have no control.'

The twins had recently come to the notice of the local police because of antisocial behaviour. Poor Judy had tried everything to discipline them. Both women knew this bad behaviour could be the start of more serious problems. There were drugs and petty crime already in the estate. Judy had a fulltime job as a nurse in the local hospital and needed the money, as Michael's cheques were becoming erratic and not sufficient to meet all the bills of a growing family.

Vera had moved in with Judy when Michael moved away to his new job abroad, initially to help with the children as Judy was on night duty. Then as she became older and less able for the cooking and care, she stayed with Judy and sold her own house. Judy was fiercely independent and would not take money from her mother. In a way, this was now a blessing as Rosebank House was known as being pricey.

Out of all the retirement homes that she had painstakingly researched this one had seemed the most appropriate, Judy felt. It was smaller than most; each resident had their own room and bathroom; there was a resident chef and physiotherapists. All other charges would be extra; hairdressing, chiropody and anything considered nonessential. Judy knew her mother well and felt that a short stay here would not do her any hurt or long-term damage.

She had also included her mother in all decisions and asked her opinion along the way. She hated having to do this, but things at home were coming to a head and she needed to be able to give her boys her full attention. She had cut down on her working hours too.

The two women got out of the car and walked into the reception area. Someone came out to take Vera's cases from the car as they entered the building.

The owner of the home, Mrs. Eva Wilson, came and warmly welcomed Vera to Rosebank and hoped that her stay would be pleasant and that she would feel at home here. If there was anything she needed, all she need do was ask.

Judy and Vera were shown to the room allocated to its newest resident, the door had a picture of a primrose and was clearly signed 'Primrose Room'.

Vera thought that was much nicer than a number. They entered the room and stood looking around. It was quite big and airy with a bed against one wall and an armchair and footrest over by the window, which looked out on the back of the house. The ensuite was also a pale lemon colour, very smart but with all the health and safety regulations; handles by the toilet, a plastic chair in the shower, more handles to guide you out of the shower. Judy started putting Vera's clothes in the built-in wardrobe which also had pull-out shelving for all her clothes and shoes. Vera's case had been in the room before they had reached it and Judy was impressed by the sensitivity and thoughtfulness of the way things were done here.

'Well, it certainly is very pretty and comfortable looking, Judy. I'm glad there are no stairs to climb too.'

'There are not many places like this, Mum. So many of the retirement homes are just old houses, big and rambling and badly adjusted to elderly people.'

Rosebank was built in a U-shaped style. Reception and entrance hall in front and dining room directly behind. The two wings contained sixteen bedrooms, eight in each. The staff quarters were in a separate building, which was once the original old house where Eva Wilson grew up. That house was now used as an extra bed unit, or sick bay, particularly for ill patients.

Vera watched her daughter as she finished putting her shoes in the lowest pullout shelf.

'We'll go and explore the dining room when I've sorted out your bathroom things, Mum. I'm dying for a cup of tea, are you? Then we must formally check in with all your medical details and dietary needs.'

'Alright love, I'd like to suss out the place while you're still here in case I get the urge to leg it.'

Judy looked at her mother anxiously and then grinned as she saw her mother's mischievous face smiling at her.

'Only joking! You know me, curious as the cat. I want to see how these places work and what the other inmates are like.'

When all was in place, Judy stood and surveyed the room. It already looked different to the one they had recently entered. Photographs on the dressing table and bedside locker made it look more like a family bedroom; her mohair shawl on the back of the armchair and about a dozen books, including photograph albums piled on the table under the window where the telephone was.

'I think it's quite a lovely room, Mum. I wouldn't half mind a month here to recuperate from my life now.'

Vera laughed. 'It is fine, no doubt about that. I'll be very cosy here love, but now let's go and get a cuppa.'

As Judy went to use the bathroom first, Vera went to the locker and deftly removed a bottle of whiskey from her handbag and stowed it beneath her now empty makeup bag. She smiled to herself and joined Vera to go to the dining room.

Chapter 2

Vera and Judy entered the dining room which was quiet enough. There were a few residents sitting at tables with obvious visitors. A young girl in a white uniform approached them and introduced herself as Susie. She was a slight Filipino girl and very friendly and smiling. She led them to a table by the window and asked them what they would like, or would they prefer to see what was on offer today? They agreed to go and have a look at the afternoon tea fare.

'Gosh, do they have this sort of spread every day?' Vera asked Susie. The girl laughed and said yes, every day. Afternoon tea was from two forty-five to four thirty every afternoon. It also coincided with visiting hours, although, she added, people could visit at any hour. There were no rigid rules here.

Judy and Vera were impressed and enjoyed their afternoon tea. Vera was feeling more at home already.

'The grub seems to be alright, Judy. I will be coming home like a little barrel unless I watch it.'

'Just enjoy it Mum. You are paying good money, just remember that. Look on it as a well-earned holiday.'

Then it was time to go to the office and fill out all the appropriate forms; all the red tape, as Vera called it.

The house manager was Miss Swift and rather different to Mrs. Wilson. She was severe looking with tightly pulled-back brown hair in a chignon that looked glued in place.

She spent the first five minutes explaining the rules which seemed sensible to the two women. There was a strict policy of no alcohol on the premises unless it was Christmas time, when wine would be served with dinner. Medication was administered in the mornings and evenings and all tablets and pills were kept in the office and given out by the nurse on duty that day.

Visitors were allowed every afternoon and there were no rigid rules about that. It was preferred though, that visitors came between the hours of two and four, but sometimes this was waived if visitors had to travel a distance.

Visits or trips to town were organised by the home and residents were not allowed to absent themselves from the home, under any circumstances.

Judy then filled in the form stating the medication that her mother was on. There were no special dietary requirements for Vera.

On their way out, another girl approached them and offered to show them the gardens. She introduced herself as Annie. She worked as a helper and was part-time. They had a leisurely stroll and there was much to admire. The roses were magnificent. Vera who used to keep a fine garden was in awe of the beauty of the place.

'Why is the place so quiet, Annie?' asked Judy.

'Most of the residents are probably still having their siesta after their dinner which is at twelve forty-five; also, the weather is quite warm for early June isn't it?'

Vera agreed and fanned her face with the brochure she had taken from the bedroom to read.

'It sure is, I think I need to sit down a while, Judy.'

Annie told them that there were wheelchairs aplenty for anyone who felt the walks were too long, even if they did not really need them. All the people there liked being out in the good weather and there were so many walks that it made sense to hop into a wheelchair if they felt a bit tired, and they were battery-operated.

'And to think I was tempted to bring my bike,' said Vera.

The departure of Judy an hour later was joyful and not at all traumatic. Judy, who thought she would be in floods of tears herself, was pleasantly surprised. Vera also thought that she would be emotional and was relieved that it went perfectly well, very civilised.

She looked around and entered a room with a brass sign on the door: The Lounge. There were lots of big armchairs and sofas around and small tables with two, three or four chairs around each. She immediately wondered whether they played bridge here. That would be a bonus indeed. One wall was devoted to books all placed on shelves within reach. She wandered over and looked at the titles and knew that there was plenty of stuff here she would enjoy reading.

She picked up a magazine and went towards the window to sit down and rest. As she sat down, a voice came from nearby.

'You'd better not sit in that bloody chair, lady, that's Sylvie's chair and she'll have your guts for garters if she finds you there.'

Vera looked around for the owner of the voice. It came from a sofa at the back of the room, in a rather dark area. An elderly man, not at all fearsome looking, was grinning broadly at her.

'Oh sorry. I just arrived today and know nothing. I'm Vera Crosbie, by the way.' She advanced and held out her hand. He did not stand up and held out his left hand, which she took.

'Hello Vera Crosbie, I am Jack Stokes and pleased to meet you. I've had a stroke so not so gentlemanly as before. The rest of 'em call me Jack Stroke.'

'Pleased to meet you Jack and thanks for the warning. Have you been here long?'

'The past three years and a bit. My daughter and sons visit now and again. They live abroad so it's not easy for them.'

Vera nodded. She now realised that her conversations with the people here would be different to the casual chats she had enjoyed before. How does one talk about handicaps and strokes and such, she wondered?

The door opened and now more people entered the room.

'It's just too hot for the garden today, isn't it?' The speaker had a loud and dictatorial voice.

The woman who said this parked herself in the seat that Vera had almost taken. So, this is Sylvie, she thought.

Several other people came in now and took up seats all around the room. Three people in wheelchairs were wheeled in. Conversation was low and there was the odd laugh. Annie came in and opened out the French doors leading to the garden.

'Is that better, everyone? This is the hottest day we have had so far, isn't it?'

There was murmured agreement.

'There should be air conditioning here, we pay enough, God knows.' Sylvie was mopping her face with a tissue and looking hot and bothered.

Then she caught sight of Vera in a chair near to Jack. 'Oh! We have a new face. Another victim drawn to the place of torture. Welcome to hell, darling.'

Jack guffawed very loudly. 'Give it a rest, Sylvie. There are no victims here unless you consider yourself the torment mistress.'

There were some suppressed giggles, quickly smothered. Vera decided to speak up for herself. She stood up and introduced herself and said how impressed she was by the beautiful gardens and house. She went around each resident holding out her hand and asking their names. Vera was not a shy person and quite confident. When she came to Sylvie she said, 'And you are Sylvie, I know, as Jack warned me not to sit in your chair.'

Again, there was muffled laughter and some coughing.

Sylvie glared at her and nodded imperiously. 'Yes, I am glad that you heeded his advice. We all have our proper places here and you would do well to learn that quickly.'

Jack came forward then, slowly, with a walking stick in his left hand. He smiled at Vera and asked her if she would like to see the recreation room. They left the lounge and he led her to a room off the far end of the dining room. It was quite large and there were various pieces of equipment there which were obviously used for exercise. He explained how they did physical exercises each morning, for those who were able; physiotherapy took place there too behind some screens and games took place there, especially during the winter when they could not go outside. Against one wall Vera noticed a piano. She felt relieved at that.

'Can anyone come in here when they wish?' she asked.

'Well, exercise has to be supervised. It's a bit like being back in a playground for five-year-olds, you know?' Jack chuckled as he said this.

On the slow walk back to the lounge, Vera thanked Jack and said, 'I hope we will be friends, Jack. I need someone to guide me around the various pitfalls I might meet.'

'Ach, there is only one, and you've already met her and stood up to her. It's a pity more of them don't; she is just a bit of a bully, used to getting her own way. No real harm in her, I think.'

'Is it a happy place on the whole, do you think, Jack?'

'Happy is a queer word, Vera, how many people are really happy, do you think?'

'Well, what about content, then?'

'I'd say most of us are more-or-less content. Sylvie is the exception. She doesn't want to be here and thinks she is missing out on life outside. Her son brought her here two years ago and she refuses to see him now. She really blames her daughter-in-law though.'

'That's sad, isn't it? Her poor son probably thought it was for her own good.'

'I'd say she and her daughter-in-law are cut from the same cloth, as they say.' Jack stopped outside the lounge and said, 'Supper is at six o'clock and then it's television or cards if you play, until bedtime.

They like us to be in our beds and lights out by ten-fifteen.'

Chapter 3

Vera woke at her usual time of six thirty. For a moment she forgot where she was and looked around at the strange surroundings. Then she remembered. As she lay in the strange but comfortable bed, she thought about the supper last night.

She had taken herself off to her room after leaving Jack and had a shower. It was a little cooler in the evening. She smiled as she relived her first experience of the communal supper. There were two tables set in the dining room, with eight places on each table. Most had been sitting when she entered, and she spied an empty place beside Jack and headed for that. There was another little lady walking in at the same time. Vera reached the chair and went to sit down. Immediately the booming voice of Sylvie protested.

'You cannot sit there, that is Ivy's place. You must sit in the newly vacant chair.'

As Vera paused, the little lady standing next to her said timidly, 'It is really alright with me, Vera. We don't have to sit in any particular place.'

Vera looked down at the sparrow-thin little person and said, 'Not at all Ivy. I have no wish to upset anyone here. After all, I have just arrived, and you are all used to being here now.'

She saw the only other empty chair and made her way to the end of the table. She saw Jack shake his head and as she caught his gaze, he rolled his eyes.

Vera decided that she would take things slowly and not get too involved in conversations until she learned the lay of the land. Keep quiet and observe, she told herself. Like being in a new school: do not plough in clumsily, hold back and see what the pecking order is.

Supper was served professionally and without pause. There was a choice of two items on the menu for supper every day, tonight it was a cooked fish supper or a salmon salad. There was muted conversation around the two tables. Sylvie could be heard clearly though, giving her opinion about everything. Vera felt that a lot of her ideas were aimed at her and made a show of being involved with her food. In fact, she felt rather tired after the journey here and the settling in and everything. She looked forward to her bed and to her usual drop of whiskey.

When supper was finished, she felt a gentle hand on her arm. It was Ivy. She smiled shyly at Vera and asked if she would like to go to the lounge. They usually all went there after supper to relax. There were card games if she wanted, Ivy explained, or there was television in the smaller room off the lounge.

Vera let herself be led off happily. She could learn the ropes from the sweet little woman called Ivy.

It seemed that nearly everyone entered the lounge and took seats there, although a few went into the television room. The evening staff wheeled the three who were wheelchair-bound. She saw Jack and a few others heading to the television room. She would not have minded seeing the news but did not want to leave Ivy or suggest anything that Ivy had not suggested herself. Listen and learn, she told herself.

Ivy led her to a table with two chairs and asked Vera if she would like to play draughts with her. Vera agreed and decided that she would make herself as amiable and quiet as possible.

Sylvie paraded over to one of the tables and boomed out loudly, 'Anyone for bridge?' She looked around the room expectantly.

A small and sprightly old man, who Vera later learned was Mr. Burrow, got up and went to join her. Vera lifted her head and looked around to see what was happening. At that moment Sylvie's eye caught hers and Vera saw the inquiry that was there. Vera looked away and continued to ponder the board in front of her. Ivy was a slow and cautious player and unless Vera made a deliberate mistake, it would go on forever.

'Do you not play bridge at all, Vera?' Sylvie's voice boomed across the room. 'You look like a bridge person.'

Vera looked up and nodded at Sylvie. 'I do yes, but tonight I am playing draughts with Ivy, maybe tomorrow. I am a bit tired, tonight.'

'Draughts, hmph,' was the only comment Sylvie made.

Vera could see that little Ivy was perturbed by this exchange and she made a mistake in her play. Her hand trembled.

'If you want to leave this and play bridge, do so, Vera, I don't mind,' she whispered

'Not at all Ivy, I am happy here. Now you be careful, you have just made a mistake. You mustn't let yourself be distracted while playing, you know.' She whispered this back to the woman, who shot her a grateful look.

Sylvie had obviously found two more players and silence descended. There were others playing cards too and some laughter erupted now and again, not loudly though as Sylvie shushed them when it got too loud.

Vera got the picture quickly. Sylvie was the big girl here and intimidated some of the residents, not all of them, however. At being shushed once too often, a man who Vera later knew as Ken, told her, 'Ah shut up, y'auld bitch, yuh.'

Vera had to turn a snort into a cough at that. Strangely though, Sylvie did not respond. She peeped up at Ivy to see how she was taking it, but Ivy was totally engrossed in her game.

By nine, Vera had had enough and pleaded tiredness to Ivy, who now mentioned watching television. She went to her room happily and got ready for bed. She was looking forward to her nightcap and got the glass from the bathroom. She opened the locker and wondered if Judy got home alright. Telephone calls were only allowed at certain times, which was understandable she thought. There was a telephone in the room but not connected to an outside line. You could ring the switchboard if you required assistance. Her hand reached into the locker and did not find what she was looking for. Bending down she peered in and removed the makeup bag that she had covered the bottle with. There was nothing there. Her whiskey had disappeared. She could not believe it! Was it somewhere else? No, she knew that she had put the bottle in the bottom of the locker. It was gone!

As she straightened up, she realised that she could not make a complaint about this. Alcohol was forbidden, for heaven's sake. She uttered a few choice words as she got into bed. She was too annoyed to read and wondered when Judy could come again and bring her some more. Of course, Judy had no idea that her mother had brought the bottle in the first place.

'Hell's bells and damnation,' she muttered to herself. I will have to watch it here. Pity it wasn't a half bottle, she thought to herself.

Chapter 4

Vera was still a bit annoyed as she mulled over her first evening at Rosebank. Somebody had seen her arrive and had visited her room while she was either in the garden, dining room or in the lounge. Then she smiled to herself. That is what I will have to do, she thought, wait for the next new arrival and raid his or her room at the first opportunity.

She remembered a story from one of her friends, a devout Christian man. When he was a student at university and understandably, short of cash he came out one night to find his bicycle had been pinched.

'What did you do Richard?' everyone asked.

'The only thing I could; I went and pinched someone else's, otherwise I wouldn't get back to my lodging.'

This had caused much merriment as they knew how particular and upstanding Richard was. Yes, Vera thought, you are driven to take opportunities when the need arises and felt a grudging admiration for the thief.

Breakfast was served from nine until ten thirty. Some of the residents had breakfast in their room, depending on their needs. People in wheelchairs had to be helped washing and dressing and there was a lot of coming and going in the dining room and corridors.

Vera looked at the menu and found she was ravenous. There was fruit, cereal, yogurt, cooked food and all sorts of breads and toast. She always believed in having a good breakfast to start the day and that the energy it provided would see her through whatever the day brought.

There did not seem to be any trouble about where one sat at breakfast. She did not see Ivy or Sylvie and sat beside a man in a wheelchair. She had not noticed him last night and so she introduced herself.

He grunted and quickly said 'I'm Bob,' and turned his attention to his bacon and egg.

Vera asked him if he had been at Rosebank for long.

'Too bloody long,' was the retort.

Vera realised that Bob was not very communicative and left him in peace after that.

The sun was shining outside, and it looked like it was going to be as nice as yesterday. Vera thought that she would take a walk after she had eaten. By now, there were more people coming into the dining room and she saw Ivy. Jack was walking with her and they greeted her as she left.

Susie was there again today and approached Vera as she crossed the foyer. The gentle girl smiled and offered to show Vera the weekly schedule of activities.

They sat outside on a bench and Susie gave her a leaflet with each day's activities printed inside.

After breakfast each day, the medications were given out. Everyone had to report to the small office on the corridor that Vera's room was on. After that there was physio for those who needed it or gentle exercises in the recreation room for all. Miss Swift, the house manager expected all able-bodied residents to avail of this. Those in wheelchairs also attended.

After that, everyone was free to walk or sit until dinner time at twelve forty-five. Tea was available in the dining room whenever anyone wanted a cup, or coffee, Susie said.

'What happens then, Susie?' asked Vera, 'Do we all have to go bye-byes until visiting time?'

Susie wrinkled her forehead, 'Bye byes?'

Vera smiled at the girl and said, 'Bed, my dear, or siesta, if you like.'

'Oh no. Only if you want to. You are free to do whatever you like, but Miss Swift thinks it is healthy to have a nap.'

Once a week there was entertainment provided by outside volunteers, usually a singsong, or storytelling. This was very popular, confided Susie. Most of the elderly loved music and they looked forward to the afternoons when this happened. Sometimes the local school children came in and performed for them, either singing, dancing or playing an instrument. This was also eagerly anticipated.

Susie asked Vera if she had any questions?

'What is happening today then, Susie?'

Susie consulted her leaflet and thought that today was free of any organised activity. Being summer, quite a lot of the local people would be on holiday as was the school. There might be something next week. It was generally announced by Miss Swift in the dining room, at mealtime.

Susie left and Vera got up to go and get her medication from the nurses' office. She thought it a bit of a waste of time. She was quite capable of taking it herself, just as she always had, but rules were rules. She knew it was a sensible rule, some people might get mixed up about whether they had taken their pills or not.

The nurse was pleasant and chatty. Her name was Maura, and she was in her fifties, if Vera was any judge of age. The medication that Vera was on was simple, a morning tablet for blood pressure and an evening one for cholesterol, plus a sleeping tablet that Vera only took if she felt she needed it. Maura asked her about her health in general and told her that if she ever wanted a chat about anything not to hesitate to drop in. She was mornings only and another nurse was on evenings. Evening medication was at seven-thirty.

On her walk around the garden, Vera thought about all she had learned so far. It seemed very well run, she had to admit. Sensible rules, friendly people. The time would surely pass quickly for her. She heard a bell pealing from the house and was ready for that. It was the bell to signal the hour of physical activity in the recreation room. She had better hurry.

As she entered the foyer again, she saw the slowly moving line of people wending their way towards the recreation room. She followed them slowly and hoped she would not stick out like a sore thumb. I will stay at the back she decided and just watch what goes on.

There were rows of straight-backed chairs arranged in two semicircles and everyone took a seat, those in wheelchairs were positioned at the end of the rows and each had a helper. This was such gentle exercise that Vera felt a bit impatient. She was used to vigorous exercise and this was an insult, she felt. She made herself calm down and listen to the instructions. The movements were all done to music, very unimaginative music. She looked around furtively. They all looked like robots, she thought. Faces were serious and movements were without energy or enthusiasm, she felt. She sighed sadly. This could be such an exciting class with a bit of imagination, she knew. Change the music for a start and what might happen? They might come alive for heaven's sake.

She suddenly felt depressed. She had never really considered being old. She had been too busy. She should have prepared for it, she thought. Here I am, sticking my arms up and out, up and out, flapping my hands like fish, lifting my feet up and down, up and down. Bending forward and back, to the side and back. On and on it went and so slowly.

At last it finished and those who wanted physio went and saw the physio and the rest trooped out slowly again.

'Did you enjoy the exercise?' Ivy came alongside Vera and asked this earnestly. Poor Vera who was feeling old now, could only nod and smile wanly.

'Is it always the same, Ivy?'

'Oh yes. It's enjoyable though, isn't it, Vera?'

Vera said, 'It is Ivy, I have been used to more vigorous movement though, so I will have to adjust.'

Chapter 5

The weeks passed slowly for Vera. She understood the routine very well now. She longed to see her daughter but knew Judy had taken the boys for a holiday, which they all needed badly. The weather was still warm and pleasant, and the roses were in full bloom.

One afternoon after dinner she strolled down to the recreation room which was deserted at this time. She made her way over to the piano and stood looking down at it. She lifted the lid and played a few notes. She was surprised; this was a well-tuned piano and not at all what she had imagined it would be. She became quite elated and pulled a chair over and sat down and played a few chords. It was in tune and had a satisfactory quality. She began to play a few pieces she had memorised over the years. She loved her music and had always had a piano. When it had been decided that she was coming here, she knew she would miss it very much. She played away happily and knew that she needed some practice. Now she knew how she would fill her afternoons. Life suddenly looked more hopeful.

After an hour, Vera got up and closed the piano. She decided she would have a cup of tea and happily made her way to the dining room. There were a couple of visitors only and the place was empty otherwise. She took her tea to a window seat and sat down feeling for the first time, totally relaxed and happy. She looked around and saw Jack had a visitor today. Not everybody got visitors she had been told. Susie was a little mine of information and told her who was who and the various foibles of the residents, not in a malicious way at all. Poor little Susie was kindness personified. She and Vera knew that having some background information often helped to understand why people were the way they presented.

'Can I join you Vera?'

The timid voice belonged to Ivy. Vera wondered if she ever took things for granted and just sat down without asking.

They spent a pleasant time just talking generalities and Vera gleaned as much as she could from Ivy's comments. No, Ivy herself did not have that many visitors. She did have a niece who came when she was in this part of the country. Christmas was the best time as rules were relaxed and there was a lovely feeling in the place. Carol singers came from outside and there was more entertainment all round. Ivy loved this holiday time.

The following afternoon after a short nap, Vera made her way to the recreation room and played the piano happily for a time. She sighed as she shut the lid of the piano and got up for an outside walk. She was startled by a quiet clapping of hands and looked around the room to see who it was. It was Jack

Stroke and another female inmate that she had not yet met.

'That was lovely Vera,' Jack said. We enjoyed listening to you playing.

'Indeed, we did,' the old lady beside him said, nodding her head approvingly.

Vera smiled at them both. She looked at the lady beside Jack. 'I don't think I have met you, have I?'

'I'm Maggie and I've been in my room quite a bit recently, but I'm better now.'

'You will have to do this often, Vera. Everyone would love to have a listen. We all love music, you know.' Maggie clapped her hands excitedly. 'I know, Jack, lets organise a party, a real singsong, wouldn't that be great?'

Jack smiled indulgently at Maggie. 'We are taking it for granted that Vera wouldn't mind entertaining us. Vera, what do you say?'

'What can I say Jack? If I can provide some or any entertainment, I would be more than willing. We can ask the powers that be, I suppose.'

'That's easy; Miss Swift can have no objection as it will be beneficial to all the residents,' Maggie said excitedly. 'I'll do it as soon as possible and let you know what happens.'

The next day there was an announcement after dinner. Miss Swift smilingly told all the diners that they now found they had a resident pianist and there would be a singsong for all at three o'clock two afternoons a week.

This was followed by excited chatter and lots of smiling faces. Miss Swift had in fact called Vera into her office and asked her advice on the singsong and if Vera would be up to two sessions a week. Vera of course agreed.

At three o'clock on the dot, most of the chairs in the recreation room were filled and the few people in wheelchairs were there too. Susie and Annie were in attendance as helpers.

Maggie was a born organiser and now found herself the centre of attention as she announced which songs they were going to sing. She and Vera had prepared a list of well known 'oldies' that Maggie felt all would know.

Vera was fortunate that she could play by ear. As a child she had always been hauled into the parlour, or sitting room when visitors came, and there was a sing song.

Soon the room was ringing with laughter and singing too. They were all a bit shy at first, but that soon disappeared, as Maggie would not take no for an answer when anyone held back. Quite a few of them had reasonable voices. Vera was quite shocked to hear Ivy sitting a solo. She had approached Vera and asked her if she could play the song, 'My Lagan Love.' It had actually been the favourite song of Vera's stepmother, so was very well known. There was silence as Ivy sang in a clear sweet voice, startling, as she was such a sparrow of a women, not a scrap of flesh on her.

She got great applause for that and sat down, flushed and happy. Then Vera had an idea. Would they like to stand up and move a little to music, no fast movements mind!

She began a medley of old-time waltzes and suddenly, they were all moving gently in time. Susie and Anne gently rolled the wheelchairs in time to the music. Vera looked over and was startled to see Bob 'Grunt', as he was called, smiling broadly and conducting the music as though he was a conductor.

Most were mobile and quickly found partners to dance with. Ivy was dancing with Sylvie and Vera and the helpers could hardly keep a straight face. Big Sylvie and little Ivy! Maggie had a strong hold of Ken, who Vera always thought of, as the rather coarse and rough man who had told Sylvie to shut up on her first evening there. Jack Stroke was gently and slowly stepping around with a woman, whose name Vera could never remember.

Mr. Burrow was dancing, serious-faced-with an equally serious-faced woman. There were women dancing with women and only a few were left sitting and they were swaying to the music and tapping their feet. After a while, they sat and started singing again. Vera did not want to overdo it.

The bell rang at four-thirty to announce the end of afternoon tea and everyone made a beeline for a cup of tea. They were all thirsty and ravenous.

Vera closed the piano and sighed happily. That had gone well indeed. She felt that she was contributing something worthwhile. As she got up, Miss Swift came into the room and congratulated her.

'What a wonderful afternoon for all,' she said, 'I am so glad that I was able to arrange this. So long as they don't get overtired or excited, Vera. You understand what I mean? We have to be careful as regards insurance and such things.'

Vera knew what she meant. Thankfully, Miss Swift had not seen the dancing. Obviously, Vera did not think the dancing was at all strenuous as she had played slowly. In fact, she thought there should be much more movement to music but was not going to state her opinion to Miss Swift. She had come to realise that Miss Swift liked to feel that it was she alone who was in charge and would not welcome too many new ideas unless she thought they originated from herself. Maggie had also been very clever the way she had introduced the topic of musical afternoons. There were no flies on Maggie.

They were still talking about it at supper and the room seemed much livelier than usual. The lounge on the other hand seemed more subdued. Many were nodding off in their chairs and by nine o'clock there was nobody in the television room or lounge.

They were all gone to bed. Vera too had gone to her room after supper. She was bushed and would have loved a tot of whiskey. She decided that she would ring Judy the following afternoon and request a bottle, she felt she deserved it.

Chapter 6

Judy visited her mother the following Saturday and brought the twins with her. Vera was delighted to see them all and hear about their wonderful holiday. Her daughter looked rested and seemed more at peace with herself. She also smuggled in a bottle of whiskey having been told it was urgently needed. They sat outside in the lovely sunshine and Vera had her big old holdall, which took the bottle of whiskey easily.

At three o'clock they all went in for afternoon tea and the boys did justice to the tasty fare. When they had finished, they went off to explore and Vera and Judy had a chance for catching up on the local gossip.

Judy broke the news that her husband, Michael was seeking a divorce and she was trying to come to terms with it. The boys knew, and it did not seem to bother them very much. It was understandable as their father had never featured very strongly in their lives. All the same, Vera felt sad for Judy. She always thought that a woman must feel rejection at being divorced.

Vera regaled her daughter about the various characters in the residence and soon had her laughing out loud.

'Honestly Mum, the names you have devised for them!'

'No, I didn't Judy, they're the names I was told by others. Poor old Bob really does grunt a lot, Ken is a lecherous old geezer, although to be fair, he has not tried anything with me yet; Maggie says that it is only a matter of time.'

'Why do they call that night attendant Sidney, 'the Snake'? Do any of them know their nicknames?'

'Well, I have had no experience of Sid the Snake, I can only tell you the stories that I've heard. It's because he is a bit sneaky. I think he was originally called Sid the Sneak and then it got a bit corrupted.'

The two women laughed. Judy was feeling much lighter at heart now that she saw that her mother had not deteriorated in any way and seemed to be enjoying the life here. Now there was a divorce to prepare for, her eldest child to settle into boarding school and the counselling seemed to be helping the twins, although they still had occasional break outs. Her work was busy and demanding too.

When her family had left, Vera walked thoughtfully to her room with her precious cargo. Where could she put it and know that it was safe? She thought about it for a while and then had an idea and smiled to herself.

At supper she relaxed happily as she answered questions from a few of the inmates. They had seen her with Judy and the boys.

Later in the lounge, she agreed to play a few hands of bridge with Sylvie. The little sprightly man called Mr. Burrow, joined them. She often wondered what his first name was. Everyone called him 'Rabbit' Burrow behind his back, but addressed him as Mister Burrow, quite formal she thought. He was a quiet and pleasant person and courteous: one of the last proper gentlemen, Vera thought.

Tonight, Ivy agreed to play bridge, and she partnered Vera. Most people were watching a football match in the television room and there was some noisy shouting at times. Sylvie did not appear to notice.

Coming up towards bedtime, Ivy made a bit of a mess of the bidding and was told off soundly by Sylvie. She had gone to four hearts having only two in her hand. Vera did the best she could, and they went down two tricks.

'Really, Ivy. What on earth got into you? You had an awful hand. Vera won't want you for a partner again.'

Poor Ivy looked shaken and apologised abjectly to Vera.

'Don't give it another thought Ivy, we all make mistakes sometimes, and after all, it is only a game. I have enjoyed the evening very much. Now I must retire, it has been a long day for me, what with my visitors.'

Vera was really looking forward to her first nightcap since she came here.

She entered her room smiling to herself. The first thing she noticed was her firmly closed locker door which she had left very slightly open. So, she thought to herself, it *is* somebody who knew and saw that I had visitors. She went through to her bathroom and confidently lifted the lid of the toilet cistern and withdrew her bottle of whiskey. She could not stop smiling at her cunningness. If Judy could see what I had to do, she thought. She sat and enjoyed her first drink in weeks, and it tasted all the better for being forbidden and so cleverly hidden. It made her feel like a young teenager.

She sat in her comfortable armchair and sipped her whiskey happily with her feet up on the footrest. There was a quiet knock on her door and Vera was surprised. She quickly put her glass down by the side of her chair and got up to open it. There were no locks on doors here as a precautionary measure. Little Ivy stood there, and Vera could see that she was upset.

'Come in Ivy, come in my dear. Sit down there on the bed. I hope that old bully did not upset you about the cards?'

'Oh no, Vera, I just feel so bad for letting you down. You are so good to play with me. I am not in your league at all. My bidding is terrible. Sylvie has tried to help me, but I cannot remember things so well now.'

'Well, don't let that woman bully you Ivy, she is quite a tyrant, isn't she?'

'Ah no Vera, you must not misjudge her, she is not like that at all really. She is my best friend here. Now that I have met you, I am lucky to have two best friends. Thank you for your patience. I just hope that I did not spoil your night.

'Not at all Ivy. We shall play again, don't worry.'

When Ivy left, Vera retrieved her drink and sat down to consider what Ivy had said. Sylvie was her best friend? How bloody strange was that? Was she so downtrodden by that woman that she was afraid to speak out about her? Vera shook her head and finished off her drink.

The next day was Sunday and was generally busy with visitors coming and going most of the afternoon. The residents who wanted to go church were brought by minibus to the church of their choice and most people went. It was a nice break from the usual daily routine too. There was also an ecumenical service for those who were ill or not attached to any church in town. This was held in the recreation room at eleven o'clock. All the residents were back in time for their dinner at twelve forty-five. Sunday's dinner was usually a choice of roasts, chicken, beef or lamb. Vera enjoyed the food here, it was superb.

She usually retired to her room to read the Sunday paper in peace and do the crosswords. If the weather was fine, she sometimes had a walk in the grounds before supper. She could never manage afternoon tea on a Sunday after the robust dinner.

On her walk today, she caught up with Maggie who was walking slowly around the rose garden. They began to chat and discuss the next afternoon of singing which usually was held on Mondays and Thursdays.

'I have a great idea Vera. I've been thinking about it for days now.' She paused and appeared to go into a daydream.

'Well what is it? Don't leave me hanging here. I want to hear about this great idea, Maggie.'

'I want us to have a dance, some night. A real dance with you playing the music. When all the staff people are busy, and we will gather in the recreation room. What do you think of that, then?'

'I doubt Miss Swift would give permission. She likes quiet evenings and wants us all in bed by ten.'

'Yes, I know that, but we have to plan it well and have it later in the night. Once it passes eleven, the night staff are usually occupied having their meal in the staff quarters and there are only two of them, you know. It's not as if they patrol the place, is it?'

Vera had no idea what the night staff did. After the medicine was given out, she never really saw any around, but then she had never left her room after bedtime.

'Let's put it to the vote, Maggie. See what the others think of the idea. It would certainly be fun.

Chapter 7

Life continued at its gentle pace at Rosebank House. Vera got used to the routine and although feeling bored at times, this generally did not last too long. Judy had brought some of her old music books and she spent as much free time going over old pieces as possible. Sometimes she had a couple of listeners when she played and sometimes not. Most had a siesta after dinner, something she had tried to cultivate earlier. But most days, she did not feel tired enough.

She closed her music books and put them on top of the piano. She felt someone at her side and looked up. There was Jack Stroke.

'We have been discussing an idea that Mad Maggie has, Vera. We would like a dance some evening here, but no doubt Sweety Swift will not allow it, so it must be done clandestinely. Will you be part of this mutiny?' He asked this with his usual cocky smile.

'Definitely, Jack. I have always been a bit wild myself and it would be a very daring thing to do. We must take care though; we can't afford any accidents.'

'It's not as if we're still teenagers, Vera, most of us can hardly walk, never mind dance. It'll be like a last fling for us all.'

'Alright Jack, we'll have a quiet word tonight in the lounge and work out which night it is to be.'

Vera was quite excited at the idea. She wondered if they could get away with it.

On her way to her room after playing the piano, she came across Mr. Burrow outside her room. She was surprised, as his room was on the other side. He smiled broadly at her and she saw why he was called Rabbit. His two front teeth were quite prominent and did make him look rather rabbit-like.

'I was looking for Jack,' he said, 'looks like he is organising a bit of a 'knees-up', have you seen him?'

'Yes, Mr. Burrow, I was just talking with him in the recreation room. Tonight, we are going to decide which night we are to be naughty.'

He laughed and rubbed his hands together. 'Great stuff, Vera, we have never had anything like this before.'

She rested in her room until supper time and read a few chapters of her book. Then she got up and took a pencil and paper and proceeded to jot down all the waltzes and foxtrots she could remember. Of course, she would have to play everything slowly, and watch out for when they needed to rest. It would not do to have a room full of corpses for the morning staff to discover. The idea made her smile.

The dining room was full of smiling people later, and there was an air of suppressed excitement. Vera hoped none of the staff noticed or were curious about it.

In the lounge when all were settled and the evening medicine given out, a sudden silence descended on the room. The people who were watching television all came out and everyone's eyes swivelled onto Maggie.

She came forward and stood in the middle of the lounge. Jack took up a position at the door and it was obvious to all that he was the look-out.

She began by saying that she had spoken to each and every person in the home, and all were in favour of the escapade. She pointed out a few sensible precautions and everyone nodded after each suggestion. Firstly, if anyone felt ill or indisposed on the said night, they must stay in their room; anyone with any worries should not feel that they must participate; secondly, all must keep their sleeping tablet until after the party. They did not want anyone falling asleep in the recreation room; and finally, everyone must arrive and depart as quietly as possible; no speaking on the way, there or back.

Vera and all the others felt that these were logical and sensible rules if they could be called rules at all.

What night are we going to go mad then?' Ken the Lech asked eagerly, leaning forward in his armchair.

Maggie put her finger on her lips and shushed the murmuring which had begun. 'There are certain days that we could not do it: I think Saturday is one,

Sunday is usually a tiring day, well for me anyway, with all these visitors in the afternoon and church in the morning, so what do you all think about Friday night?'

Ivy put up her hand timidly and Maggie nodded to her. 'Maggie, I feel that Friday is a good night as the night staff are usually relaxed, and it's known that they play cards in the staff room then.'

Ken the Lech leaned forward and said very loudly, 'I agree with Ivy. The staff are always more relaxed on Fridays, I've heard them call it Happy Friday.'

Maggie glared at him. 'Do you have to speak so loudly Ken? We must be quiet about this or we could land in a load of trouble.'

Ken had the grace to look guilty and muttered an apology.

After a show of hands, it was decided that the following Friday night would be IT. Maggie also suggested that when talking about it, they must refer to it as the Christmas stocking, or if they forgot that , anything to do with Christmas, just so as nobody would have any inkling of what they were talking about. This suggestion caused a lot of smiles, the secrecy of the matter had a childlike appeal to all these elderly citizens.

Jack Stroke, Ken and Jack O'Hare, known as Jack Other, had a few specific ideas which they did not discuss with the rest. They were seen together in the coming days in the dining room having afternoon tea but sitting closely together and deep in conversation.

On Thursday evening in the lounge, Maggie again took the floor and gently clapped her hands for attention. Everyone stopped what they had been doing and silence descended.

'Now listen up, tomorrow is 'Christmas' and I want you all to retire to bed in dribs and drabs, not all together, that might attract attention. We must all be in our beds by ten, but ready to come alive by twelve. If we all have a siesta on Friday afternoon, we won't be too tired, or in danger of falling asleep and missing it. Any questions, anyone?'

'What if one of the night staff checks us in bed?' Ivy ventured this question. Now that the event was a day away, she was nervous.

Jack Stroke laughed, 'Ivy dearest, you must make your bed *look* as if you are in it. Put your spare pillow under the covers to look like a body. Nobody is going to check that it's you, and you will appear to be fast asleep.'

After that, the tension in the room dispersed and games resumed, and people went back into the television room.

Tonight, it was poor Rabbit Burrow who got it hot and heavy from Sylvie.

'Really, Mr. Burrow! That was a dreadful hand you played. There were two winners on the table you know, and we should not have gone down a trick.'

Poor Mr. Burrow looked ashamed and if there had been a burrow handy would surely have crawled down with speed. All he could do was to shake his head and apologise to his partner.

Ivy and Vera were playing opposite them and little Ivy said to Sylvie, in his defense, that Mr. Burrow was obviously thinking about Friday night and was distracted.

Vera was surprised when Sylvie agreed with Ivy and looked a little more kindly at Rabbit, and patted his hand.

'Of course, that was it. We are all up in a heap with the excitement, aren't we?'

Mr. Burrow nodded his head and agreed that it was the reason he played badly.

As Vera left the lounge for bed, she noticed the three men talking quietly in a corner. She had noticed them a few times during the week and wondered what on earth was so interesting and obviously all absorbing for them to be in cahoots all the time. Maybe she would ask Jack Stroke as he was more approachable than the other two.

In the foyer Sid the Snake was leaning on the counter reading a newspaper. He nodded briefly as Vera passed. She realised then, how unobservant she was, she was never aware of her surroundings or who was about the place. It was different in the afternoons, then Susie and Annie were so conspicuous. Maybe it was because they all had more dealings with them, and they were both so friendly and nice.

Chapter 8

Friday was raining hard most of the day and nobody could go outside for a walk. The day dragged by slowly and people were feeling edgy waiting for night to fall.

At last, supper was over, and all headed to the lounge. Jack and Ken were moving around quite a lot and seemed anxious. Vera looked at them over her reading glasses as she sat playing draughts with Ivy.

'What's eating them?' she muttered under her breath.

Ivy looked over her shoulder. 'They look as though they are planning something, don't they?'

At nine o'clock, Maggie coughed repeatedly and got their attention. She nodded towards the door of the lounge. A few people got up and said goodnight to the rest. Half an hour later, another four left and it continued until Maggie and Jack were left. They went out and looked around as they went. They went into the dining room and made a cup of tea to take to their rooms. Nobody else was there. Sid was on Maggie's wing and bringing a carafe of water into Bob the Grunt's room.

As Maggie passed him, she said 'this wet weather has us all floored, Sid.'

He grinned at her and told her that the weather forecast for the weekend was better and that they would be all out golfing tomorrow.

Maggie glared at him and said, 'yeah, right! Like we always play golf on Saturday!'

He smirked at her and said, 'well I will, for sure.'

Silence descended on the residence and Sid and the tall Sri Lankan man, Mano, looked forward to their night, playing cards. They were hurriedly finishing their duties and rounds on the wings.

Jack was the last up and had dropped into the staff sitting room before heading to his room. He was smiling to himself as he went.

Midnight came and slowly all the bedroom doors opened, and a procession of motley dressed men and women made their way softly and carefully to the recreation room. Jack and Mr. Burrow had got Bob into his wheelchair and were carefully wheeling him down. Two other ladies were being wheeled by more able-bodied people. They were the last to enter the room. The doors were closed, and curtains drawn so not a chink of light could be seen from the grounds. The Zimmer frames had been taken away from the physio corner and were left at various places around the room. The chairs were arranged by the piano in two semicircles. The space was freed up for dancing.

Vera started up softly with an old-time waltz. At first, there was little conversation. It was as if they were afraid of being heard. This disappeared after a couple of waltzes and soon they were chatting away, although not too loudly. They were all dancing, even if it was just a slow walk, like Jack Stroke and a few others who were not as spritely on their feet. Sylvie and Ivy were really going at it and were good dancers. Sylvie led of course but she was a graceful dancer, and very light on her feet, despite her largeness. Ivy looked as if she was in heaven. Maggie and Ken made a handsome couple even if Maggie had to push Ken away at times as he tried to get closer.

Bob Grunt looked happy and was able to push his chair around and about. When he tired of this he stayed by Vera and conducted.

Sylvie came up to Vera at some stage and demanded more modern music.

'Vera, can you play some Abba music? We need a bit more fun stuff.'

Vera was surprised but immediately obliged and soon they were all moving energetically to "Waterloo". Maggie was having a ball. She had left Ken and got another man to his feet, Jack Other. He had obviously been a jiver in his day and was soon twirling Maggie around and attracting attention. Ivy was now dancing with Mr. Burrow and Sylvie had been claimed by Ken.

The night sped by and soon it was two o'clock in the morning. Vera felt exhausted with the non-stop playing and thought it a good time to finish. Jack Stroke agreed, and they all sat and had some quiet time before they gradually drifted back to their rooms. Jack and Mr.-Burrow wheeled Bob back to his room, and Vera and Maggie left last and tried to make the room look as it had been, before the hooley. The women murmured about what a great night it had been, and Maggie said she was really looking forward to the next one. Vera thought the residents might need a bit of time to recover. Maggie disagreed.

'Could we not make this a regular thing on Fridays?'

'No, we mustn't get too used to it in case one of the staff finds out. We'll play it by ear. We can discuss it at our next singsong.' Vera decided to be cautious.

Maggie said that could not happen, with staff usually being present at the singsongs, it would have to be in the lounge at nighttime.

Vera was too tired to say anything and the two ladies walked slowly up to their rooms.

The next morning there was not a sound on either wing. It was ten o'clock before anyone appeared for breakfast. They all looked a bit bleary-eyed. Jack sat next to Vera and asked if she had remembered to take her sleeping tablet?

'Jack, I could have slept standing up I was that tired. I did not need any tablet. Did you?'

Jack lowered his voice. 'I have not taken a tablet all week Vera, I need them for a different purpose. Now lady, anytime you don't take your sleeping pill, keep it for me and I will put it to good use.' He smiled at her.

'What do you mean, good use?'

He put his face a little closer. 'I had to make sure the two young lads had a good night's sleep and would not start wandering around the place.' He winked at her.

'Jack! Don't tell me you knocked them out with sleeping pills.' Vera was shocked.

'Agh not at all! Just made them a bit groggy. I added it to their pot of coffee. Won't do them a bit of harm.'

He laughed and after a while so did Vera.

Later that morning, there seemed to be a lot of people queueing up to see the physiotherapists. Maggie had a bit of a limp, Vera noticed. She asked her later if all was well and Maggie replied, 'never better'.

Chapter 9

On the minibus taking the residents to church on Sunday morning, there was lots of chatter. The word Christmas came into a lot of the talk. Vera smiled around at all these new friends of hers. They had enjoyed the evening so much and it had introduced a new atmosphere into the home. Everyone was much chattier and friendly.

Ivy sat beside Vera on the bus. She confided that her hips had been at her since the dance. Vera turned and looked at her, smiling.

'Ivy dearest, we should not be dancing at our age, in all probability. We are asking for trouble, don't you think?'

'Oh no Vera! Don't say that! It was wonderful and I don't care about the pains and aches afterwards. I felt like a young one again. I am not really complaining. I should not have told you at all. We must do this again and again. It makes such a difference to the life in here. You don't understand because you are not here that long.'

Vera patted Ivy's hand. 'We shall my dear, never fear. We just have to leave a certain amount of time to recover, you know?'

'Ivy confided quietly, 'it has made such a difference to poor Sylvie, Vera, you'll never know how much.'

Vera could not understand that remark. "Poor Sylvie", indeed. She could not see anything at all poor about the woman. At every opportunity she let people know about her late husband, and the important man that he had been, back in his time--- a bank manager and on the boards of various financial institutions. Vera let it pass and they both resumed looking out the window at the rural scenes passing by.

'What about you, Ivy? Were you happily married?'

Ivy hesitated and then said in a rush, 'Of course, Vera, but I had no children.'

Vera sensed that she had intruded into a place where she had no business intruding

'Ivy dear, children are very much over-rated. I'm sure it didn't bother you or your late husband.'

Ivy did not reply and only sighed deeply.

Dinner was at the usual time. The residents were delighted to see Mrs. Eva Wilson joining them in the dining room.

Every fourth Sunday she did this and chatted to each and every one of the residents. They really appreciated this and had great admiration for Mrs. Wilson. She was warm and very approachable, and everyone just opened up to her, and felt better when she spoke to them. She made them feel as if she believed they were important and that created a good feeling in them all. After all, they were all old, and work was a distant memory. Their expertise in their various former lives was soon forgotten somehow and a lot of them felt inferior and somehow not worth anything anymore.

Children they had once nurtured and educated were someway removed from them now and a few people felt that their children now regarded them with amusement and treated them as you would treat young children.

Eva approached Vera and pulled a chair to sit beside her as coffee was served.

'Vera, we are so thrilled that you can entertain the residents so well. I have had such great reports from everyone, and the staff has noticed a difference in the mood of the residents. Singing is really a wonderful therapy, isn't it?'

'I think music in general is a blessing from above, Mrs. Wilson. It is mentioned in all the medical journals that I have come across, as a most beneficial entertainment. It lifts the mind up and beyond oneself, I think'

As Mrs. Wilson went on to praise the talent that Vera had, Vera suddenly had a vision of the oldies jiving and moving energetically to the music of "Waterloo" and had to suppress a smile. She wondered what Eva would have thought if she had witnessed that.

Vera, as usual went up to her room after Sunday dinner and read the newspaper she had bought in town. There were newspapers provided at the home every day and she always tried to get one, mainly for the crosswords. She lay on her bed and relaxed and had a small whiskey. Life was not bad she decided.

About an hour later she woke with a start. What had wakened her so abruptly? She sat up and listened intently. There it was again. An alien sound, she thought. She got up and went to her door and opened it quietly, listening intently. There it was again. It sounded like someone crying. She stuck her head out and looked up and down the wing. There was nobody about at this hour. Sunday was always a siesta day after the big lunch. If visitors arrived for someone, a day staff member would go and rouse the person if they were in their room.

Vera had no shoes on and went down the corridor to try and identify which room the sound was coming from. It was from the Daffodil Room, which was Sylvie's. She stopped outside and wondered what she should do. Should she interfere with That Woman?

She did not have to decide. The door opened as she stood there wondering and little Ivy emerged, closing the door behind her quietly. She jumped when she almost bumped into Vera.

Vera looked at her with a question in her eyes. Ivy just shook her head and put her finger on her lips. She took Vera's arm and led her back the way she had come. At Vera's door she stopped.

'Don't worry Vera, she is alright. I will explain later.' Again, she put her finger on her lips and went off to her own room.

Vera went into her room bemused. Why was Sylvie crying? What was the special relationship with Ivy? She felt very curious and knew that she would have to ask Ivy as soon as possible what it was all about.

Back in her room, she sat in her armchair and thought about her life here in Rosebank House. Just when she felt that she was settling in and knew everybody, something like this happened and she realised that she was still an outsider and that there was a lot she did not know and understand. All these people had been together for longer than she, and they knew all the shifts of mood in each other and probably knew everyone's background too.

Vera felt that Ivy was the key to understanding the others. She was such a quiet soul, but she picked up on things and people confided in her, she felt. It was not that she was nosy about the others or their lives, it just made her feel a stranger still when she knew they were all well acquainted with each other.

Everyone was protective of Ivy and she was understanding of that. There was something childlike about Ivy that demanded protection. Sylvie was the direct opposite. Vera had known many women like her, from schooldays onwards. Big bullying women, who usually terrorised the most timid and quiet ones.

She sighed and threw her unfinished crossword on her bed. Her brain was too busy to concentrate on that.

She felt most comfortable around Jack Stroke. He was uncomplicated and normal. With Jack she could talk easily, at any time and forget that she was in an old-aged home.

It was difficult to communicate with Bob Grunt; Mr. Burrow was so circumspect that she felt she must always watch what she said, and she had only heard stories of Ken the Lech so could not really judge the man. She felt she must strive harder to understand these characters that surrounded her and now made up a good part of her life.

Chapter 10

It was Monday and Vera received a letter from Judy. Everything was progressing well in her life. Her divorce was going ahead, and it all seemed straightforward enough. She had a good solicitor. It now was apparent that Michael had another woman in his life, and this was the reason he suddenly wanted a divorce. The solicitor had laid the expectations before Judy and it appeared to be a generous settlement to her. Vera was surprised. If he could afford this now, why were his previous cheques so inadequate?

She sighed as she put the letter away. Why was life so complicated nowadays? Her marriage had been straightforward enough. Her husband had been a hardworking man who loved his employment and his family. No, she would not start reminiscing about that life that was now well over. Going backwards in her thoughts always left her feeling sad, and out of sorts.

She made her way to the recreation room after medicines were given out. A bit of exercise before her morning gallop around the garden would cure her.

As she entered the room, Maggie waved over at her. The physiotherapist came in and went to turn on her music. Maggie got to her feet and brought something she had in her hand up to the girl. A conversation ensued. The rest of the waiting residents wondered what was being discussed. After a few minutes, the young physio nodded, smiling at Maggie. She inserted the disc which Maggie had given her. As the music of Abba emerged, everyone clapped delightedly. The exercises today were performed with great energy and gusto. Paula, the physio was quite startled. What had happened to the usually sedate and halfhearted attempts at exercise?

Those on their feet were swaying along and moving their hips, which she had never noticed before. Bob the Grunt was waving his arms about and grinning madly. Ken the Lech was standing by Vera and leering at her at every opportunity. She did not notice him at all, being preoccupied by Judy's letter. She had not had the chance to dance, being the pianist, so today she moved as much as possible. She loved rhythm to music and had once been a good dancer.

After two energetic dances or exercises to the music, everyone needed a rest and sat down on the nearest chairs. As she turned to find one, Vera felt a hand give her a quick pat on her bottom. Turning, she saw Ken grin at her. She quickly moved across the room and found a seat beside Ivy and Sylvie. She was not going to put up with his unwanted advances, aged as she was.

Paula congratulated everyone on their efforts but warned them not to overdo it. They all clapped at the end of the session and moved off to have their morning cup of tea or stroll in the garden. Some of the less mobile retired to the television room to relax.

Bob the Grunt came alongside Vera, pushed by Susie. She felt her hand being taken and thought that it was Ken. Bending down to hear what he said, she smiled and nodded.

She had a quick cup of coffee and went outside to the garden. It was a fine and sunny morning and Bob was parked alongside a woman in a wheelchair, Vera thought that her name was Maisie. Vera sat down beside him and waited for him to tell her his plan. Eventually he turned and looking at her seriously told her his story.

He had been a drummer in a band when he was a younger man. He really missed his drums. What he wanted now, was to be able to accompany Vera when she played the piano. That stumped her. Where on earth would they find a drum here? She was told that his friend would be able to bring in his drums when he next visited. Nothing *too* big, as it would create too much noise. Would she agree to that? Vera had no option but to agree. Bob nodded contentedly and grunted.

Vera got up and went for a stroll around the rose garden, which was so full of colour this month, coming nearer the end of the summer. She felt sad as she thought of not seeing them again during the cold months.

She heard the patter of footsteps behind her and turning, saw Ivy coming towards her. She was rather breathless.

'Did you talk to Bob, Vera? And what do you think?'

'I did indeed, Ivy. I had to say yes to the poor man, he was so serious about it.'

Ivy gave a sigh and smiled at Vera. 'I am so glad. He is such a darling and never asks for anything, you know?'

'It is hard to get to know him, Ivy, he never says much, only grunts. Why do you say he is a darling?'

'Oh Vera! He has had a sad life but never complains. He was a great drummer years ago. All my friends and I used to dance and loved the band he played in. He was such a good-looking fellow. All us girls had a crush on him. However, he married a girl who really did not appreciate him. She later ran off with the guy on the bass guitar, and they broke Bob's heart, I'd say. Later he got diabetes and two years ago had a double amputation, did you know that?'

Vera had not known and was shocked and saddened for Bob. Now she would not be annoyed at his grunting. He had good reason. How little we know of other people's suffering. If we had any idea, we would be much less judgmental she knew.

'What about Sylvie, Ivy? Why was she crying, can you tell me?

Ivy hesitated and looked uncertain.

'Look, you don't have to tell me Ivy. You must think I am a nosy busybody; it's just that I do not understand how you are so friendly with her. To me she appears quite unpleasant.'

Ivy nodded. 'Someday I will explain, Vera, I don't want to do that just now, if you don't mind.'

Vera turned to Ivy. 'You are a true friend Ivy, and I am so pleased we get on together. You must never tell me anything you are not comfortable with. I respect you very much. You have integrity, which is a rare thing'

Ivy had appeared puzzled at first at Vera's comments, but finally smiled at her and thanked her for her understanding.

The singsong was well attended that afternoon. The only person missing appeared to be Sylvie. Maggie had a list of songs that they all knew. She had done a bit of homework in her free time and asked about favourite songs and who would like to sing.

Susie and Annie also enjoyed these sessions. Now and again other staff members would appear and there was a lot of coming and going. Even Sweety Swift sat in occasionally and could be heard singing along.

Today as the session finished and there was a mass exodus towards the dining room, Vera was surprised to find Eva Watson [WILSON] in the recreation room. She smiled and walked towards Vera.

'I hope you enjoyed our singing, Mrs. Watson', said Vera, closing the piano.

'Indeed, I did, Vera. I want to ask you something. Do you think it would be possible to get a choir together with all the residents? I am thinking about Christmas when it would be so welcome and seasonal. We always have a big Christmas tree here and presents are distributed on Christmas morning. I just thought it would give them all something to prepare and look forward to as well as adding to the festive season.'

'That is a wonderful idea, Mrs. Watson. I think it would be very possible and we can start preparing as soon as autumn comes.'

'Yes Vera, it is really important that everyone has something to look forward to. It is mentally stimulating and good for overall health.'

Vera was delighted at the prospect of getting a choir together. It would be stimulating for her also. She had a fear of getting bored and being non-productive. If she succumbed to that, she knew it would be a downhill journey to the end.

Chapter 11

The residents were getting restive again and wanted to know when the next dance would be held. Which Friday?

Maggie and Vera conferred with Jack Stroke and Bob. They had not had a dance evening for three weeks due to one reason or the other. Now they were more than ready for their second one. Bob had his drums brought into his possession and drumsticks and was itching to go.

Jack went round as usual and tried to collect a few sleeping tablets to keep the night staff happy and asleep. Maggie asked for favourite numbers and had a list for Vera.

Sylvie had been very quiet the past couple of weeks and Vera asked Ivy if she was sick. Ivy was rather non-committal and just said that Sylvie needed rest. Vera for some reason felt disappointed. She knew Sylvie had enjoyed the first dance evening very much and looked happier than before. Vera decided to approach her herself and ask her to come.

The opportunity arose after dinner on Wednesday. Coming out of the dining room, she waited behind for the woman to catch up and then asked her how she was keeping.

'I'm very well, thank you, Vera.'

'Are you going to come on Friday night to our special evening Sylvie. It was so enjoyable the last time, wasn't it?'

'It was, indeed, Vera. I will make a decision by lunch time tomorrow.'

Vera smiled at her and said: 'Great. I know that Ivy will enjoy it more if you are present.'

At the singsong on Thursday, Vera mentioned Eva Watson's idea of a choir for Christmas. There was a flutter of excitement among the more aware of them. The few patients with dementia would always go along with the majority anyway, and they, more than anyone else appreciated singing. Their whole demeanour changed after a singsong, there was a light in their eyes and a lightness in their step.

Ivy was walking on air. Sylvie had agreed to come to the Friday special. The usual routine was adhered to, early to bed and up again at midnight. It reminded Vera of when they were children and had midnight feasts, thinking their parents did not know.

Everyone assembled as before. Bob the Grunt was smiling broadly tonight and showed off his drums proudly. Jack Other warned him not to beat them too loudly, just in case.

Vera was in fine form and started with the usual slow waltzes. Gradually they warmed up and demanded more jazzy stuff. Ivy did not leave Sylvie's side Vera noticed. The Zimmer frame people danced together and were careful in their movements.

Maggie went mad as usual and danced with all who asked her. However, she made a point of dancing with Ken the Lech only once, much to his chagrin. She danced a lot with Mr. Burrow who was a good dancer. Ken could not get near Ivy or Sylvie either and had to make do with a couple of arthritic women who could not move so freely. Bob was superb on the drums and played with great concentration.

Then Sylvie requested a tango and that really made the night. It was so hilarious. Vera was reminded of the film "Some like it hot" when Jack Lemmon danced the tango with Joe E. Brown. Little Ivy was so serious as she followed Sylvie's lead and the tallness of Sylvie with little Ivy was comical. The tears were rolling down Vera's face as she finally brought the music to a dramatic end, with an impressive drum roll from Bob. Everyone clapped enthusiastically until Maggie shushed them.

It was even better than the first dance night, and everyone staggered off to bed at two o'clock with happy grins on their faces. Bob thanked Vera for allowing him to play with her. Jack Stroke came and slapped them both on the back and congratulated them. He pushed Bob back to his room and Vera went on to her wing. She was surprised to see Ken outside her door and wondered what he wanted.

'Vera, that was a wonderful night altogether. You do a wonderful job, so you do. What about a nightcap then? I know you like a little drop. I'm right, aren't I?'

'How do you know that Ken? I thought alcohol was forbidden on the premises.'

He smirked and opened his hand and showed a half bottle of whiskey.

She opened her bedroom door to pass through, but immediately Ken came over and she knew he intended to enter too. She stopped still and looked at the man who had a silly grin on his face.

'No Ken, *my* bottle of whiskey is long gone. I'm very tired so if you don't mind, I'm going to bed.' She gave him a severe look and was pleased to see the man take a step back.

She wished there were a lock on her door. She knew she had a panic button but the thought of causing a drama did not appeal to her. She stood for a minute with her back against the door but heard a door opening further along the and knew it was Ken's room. He was next to Sylvie.

Her sleep was light and broken and she woke heavy headed. It was not possible to totally relax after that confrontation. She wondered who she could mention it to; maybe Jack Stroke, he would be able to offer some advice perhaps. For all she knew, Ken might try it on with many of the women here. A word in his ear from a strong man might make him behave. It would be difficult to tell one of the night staff or anyone for that matter. How could she explain how she met him at that time of night, when they were all supposed to be in bed by ten thirty?

She brooded about it over her breakfast. Today would be busy with visitors coming. Judy had phoned during the week and told her that she would not be coming to visit this week

Mr. Burrow approached her and told her how much he enjoyed the evening. He hoped that she was not too tired as she had to play non-stop for two hours. She was touched at his concern and admitted to being a little tired, although in her heart she knew that it had nothing to do with the entertaining.

'You should do what I do,' he told her. 'Twice a week I have a back massage with the physio. It really works wonders.'

Vera thought that she might do that and after breakfast went to the recreation room and made an appointment for a massage on Monday morning.

Everyone was quiet that morning. She did not see either Ivy or Sylvie at breakfast. She guessed the dancing took its toll on them all and smiled to herself. It was a good sort of tiredness, she thought, and the exercise was what they needed.

She got the chance she was looking for in the garden. There was Jack Stroke sitting on the bench under the big old oak tree. She made her way over and joined him.

'Saturdays are different after the dancing, Vera. I don't think anyone feels like doing much. I don't, that's for sure.'

Vera gently broached the subject that was on her mind. She told Jack of her experience with Ken. She barely started when Jack began to nod his head.

'I know exactly what you are going to tell me Vera. He tries it on all the women here. I thought you would have been complaining before now, but then I thought, sure, maybe she enjoys a bit of flirtation.'

His eyes were twinkling as he said this, and Vera knew that he was joking.

'Well, Jack. It was not the sort of thing I was expecting at two in the morning and just outside my bedroom. To be honest, it was a bit intimidating Jack.'

'What do the other women do about it? Can they complain or are they frightened to?'

'Oh, my dear, many have complained, and a night staffer usually has a word and then there is peace for a few weeks.'

Vera did not say anything. She believed it was probably a once-off incident.

Jack patted her arm and told her not to worry about it. 'There is something you can say that will prove most effective, Vera.'

'Really Jack? What exactly can I say?'

Jack turned to face her and said: 'if he bothers you again Vera, just ask him if he would prefer to move back to Broadlands. That'll put the wind up him.'

'What or where is Broadlands?'

'It's the place he was in before coming here. A right tough place for people like that. He only got in here because of some high-up politician pulling strings.'

As he said this he grinned and winked at her.

'I will certainly do that then, Jack. Also, I have been worried about Sylvie, I heard her crying a while back. Is she mentally stable, do you think?'

Jack turned to her abruptly. 'Sylvie? She is as sharp as scissors, lady. She ruled her husband's life very ably and he was a sharp man too. It was unfortunate that he had certain inclinations, as they say. She was left with a lot of his debt to clear when he died suddenly.'

'Oh dear. I did not suspect anything like that. She loves to boast about her husband, doesn't she?'

'Ah well, we who know her background understand. It's a sort of loyalty, isn't it? She would not like anyone to think she was not the wife of an important man, at the same time.'

Vera agreed with Jack. For someone like Sylvie, it would be natural to want to keep up the pretence.

Chapter 12

There were a lot of visitors that Saturday afternoon. However, the rain came down after dinner and it was too wet to go outside. The dining room was full, and all the tables were occupied, and it was a noisy time.

Vera had a knock on the door at three o'clock. She put down her crossword and rose to answer it. It was Susie to say that she had a visitor. Vera was surprised. She was not expecting anyone. She wondered who it might be, and Susie thought it was probably a grandson. So it was. Standing awkwardly in the foyer was her eldest grandson, Charlie. She hugged him warmly and said he was a welcome sight.

They sat at a little table in the foyer as the noise was loud coming from the dining room. Susie thoughtfully brought a tray with two cups of tea and a plate of scones and cakes. It was a joyful reunion being so unexpected. He had got the train by himself and Vera realised that he had grown up a lot since she last saw him. She soon got all the news out of him and knew why he had undertaken the journey.

'Granny, can you speak to Mum about this? I am worried as I'll be going to boarding school in a couple of weeks '

Vera sipped her tea and tried to think clearly. Charlie had said that his mother had started dating again recently, even though the divorce was not finally through. She was rather shocked to hear this. It was not like Judy. She could imagine the three boys being traumatised by a new man coming to the house regularly.

'It is not as though he is likable, Granny. He is not, and the twins already hate him. What will they be like if it continues? Supposing she wants to marry him, what'll we do?'

Vera did not know what to say, she also felt traumatised.

Charlie leaned forward and asked his granny if she could possibly come back home? This was very awkward, and she was stuck for words, for once.

Vera patted the boy's hand. 'I will certainly have a good chat with her and find out what all this is about, trust me, Charlie. It could be reaction to the divorce and perhaps she is in shock still.'

Poor Charlie looked miserable and worried. Vera was annoyed and angry with her daughter. Why was she doing this now, at this time? Charlie was at a difficult age, ready to start secondary school, the twins were in counselling. Hell's bells! What was wrong with Judy?

The rain had stopped, and Vera suggested a walk with Charlie around the grounds. She tried to distract the boy by telling him about the residence and the occupants thereof. She tried to make him laugh and made up a few funny stories about them. He looked at his watch at four and said he must go and catch a bus to bring him to the train station.

She hugged the boy tightly and assured him that she would be in touch with his mother very soon and would do all she could to sort things out.

Vera returned to her room. She sat and looked out the window pondering the turn of events at home and wondered just what she could do about it. She felt quite helpless.

She decided that she would ring Judy tonight after supper and hoped that she was not on night duty, but she doubted that she would be.

She had a light supper and hardly heard a word that Jack Stroke or Ivy said. They did not seem to notice her preoccupation.

Sylvie passed by the table when they were almost finished. 'Don't forget bridge tonight, Vera, you and I are playing against Ivy and Mr. Burrow.'

Vera had completely forgotten. How would she ever concentrate on bridge after that visit? She would not be able to make a phone call after nine o'clock. She did not want this call to be hurried. She needed time to broach the subject without having to look at her watch. She would have to wait until tomorrow, she thought. Another sleepless night she felt.

Ivy was not nervous about playing bridge tonight. She liked Mr. Burrow and he was kind to her. She played quite well when she was not nervous, she knew.

The evening dragged on and Vera felt increasingly miserable. She could not concentrate at all and made numerous mistakes. Sylvie was getting more and more irate.

'Vera, what is the matter with you tonight? You passed my two club opening, for heaven's sake. If this is going to continue you should consider giving up bridge.'

'I apologise Sylvie, my mind is not on the game. Do you mind if I retire now?'

'I certainly do, we have to finish this rubber whatever happens, then you can go.' She glared at Vera and Ivy looked anxiously at Mr. Burrow who did not seem to be aware of any tension at the table.

It only got worse and Vera felt mortified. Mr. Burrow patted her hand and told her not to worry, it was only a game. Sylvie glared and gathered up the cards, her lips tightly closed.

Vera left the lounge and went slowly to her room. A few minutes later there was a knock and Ivy entered. She looked anxiously at Vera. 'Something has happened to you, hasn't it? I know something is wrong, my dear friend. Can I help at all?'

Vera shook her head despondently. 'Just a family hiccup Ivy. Nothing anyone can do, at this moment.'

'I am always here Vera, to listen if that is any consolation.'

Vera thanked her and told her she might need someone to listen to her in the coming days.

She got ready for bed and poured herself out a small drop of whiskey. It was almost gone, and she wondered when she would be able to get more.

Would Judy be visiting soon? She surely needed to tell her mother about this mystery man in her life. Vera knew that sleep would not come easily now and prepared herself for a restless night. Anyway, she was not tired at all. Weary and heavy headed, but not physically tired.

At three o'clock she was still awake and decided to go and make a cup of tea in the dining room. She put on her slippers and dressing gown and softly opened her door. As she went into the dining room, she met Sid the Snake coming against her. He smiled and asked: 'having trouble sleeping, dearie?'

She hated being called that. She nodded briefly and went in and quickly made a cup of tea. There was an urn with constant boiling water. She picked a foil wrapped biscuit from the box on the counter, and slowly returned to her room. Sid had disappeared, thankfully.

She sat on her armchair and sipped her tea. She heard a door nearby closing and wondered who else was awake and sleepless.

There was a further bit of noise she thought. What was happening and where? It was not too loud, but any noise at that time of night was surely strange. She sat still and finished her tea and biscuit. She began to think that all was quiet again when she heard voices arguing. She got up and opened her door looking up the corridor. Where was the noise coming from? She waited silently and wondered if she should alert anyone. There was a further sort of thump and then the door of Sylvie's room opened, and a figure emerged. Someone in a dressing gown. She thought it looked like Ken and watched as he walked on towards the end of the corridor. He did not look behind him. He paused at his door to open it and Vera ducked back into her room, closing the door quietly.

She was in shock. What on earth was that man doing in Sylvie's room at three thirty in the morning? She had quite forgotten the family trouble that had been bothering her earlier with this new mystery

She fell asleep deeply about five thirty or six o'clock and did not wake until after nine. She lay in bed wondering what day it was. Sunday, she realised, and knew she could not think of going to church or anywhere else for that matter. She was exhausted.

Eventually she got up and went down to the dining room. Ivy and Jack were sitting with Jack Other and having a good big breakfast. It made Vera nauseous to even think of eating.

Ivy looked at her and noticed her pallor. 'Vera, you don't look well. You should stay home today, and I will get you your Sunday paper, alright?'

Vera nodded and smiled wanly. 'Thank you, Ivy, you're right. That's what I will do.

Chapter 13

The talk on the bus was about the Friday night dance or Christmas as they all called it. The couple of staff who accompanied the crowd of residents did not really notice. They were all mainly involved in their own conversations.

Maggie was sitting with Ivy and the vision of Sylvie and Ivy doing the tango still had her enthralled. She could not stop talking about it. Ivy smiled contentedly and did not say much. Maggie was a chatterbox. Ivy was glad, as she was a bit worried about Vera and wondered whether the piano playing was too much for her. She intended to have a good chat with her after they returned.

She worried about Sylvie too, she had not emerged from her room this morning and did not answer the knock on her door. Ivy knew better than to disturb her. She had her moments when she wanted her privacy.

Ivy sighed and thought about her life now. It was so different. She was not one to complain. She had never had so many friendly people around her and such good food in her life before Rosebank House. She liked the people there generally. She knew that some were deteriorating year by year and guessed she would go the same way. It was just a matter of waiting, wasn't it?

Maggie nudged Ivy and said, 'wake up Ivy. You have not heard a word of what I have said, have you?'

'Sorry Maggie. My mind is all over the place. Do you ever wonder what we're doing here? Waiting for the end, isn't it?'

Maggie looked at her friend in alarm. 'What has got into you all of a sudden, Ivy? We are living, aren't we? And in a nice enough place. We are enjoying life and it's just got a whole lot better recently I think.'

Ivy sighed deeply. 'We are approaching the last exit on the roundabout, aren't we? Sometimes I just wonder about everything, that all.'

'Ah, that is only natural Ivy. All of us here get those moments.' Maggie laughed and poked Ivy with her elbow 'In another year or two we'll be like those old dears up front. We won't remember anything much of day to day affairs and won't that be a blessing?'

They did not realise that their conversation had been overheard. Jack Other was sitting across from the two women on the outside seat. Now he leaned in and said in a conspiratorial whisper. 'Ladies, the time is coming soon when the knock on the door will come on people's seventieth birthday and that will be that. They won't be allowed to take up space any longer. We've done rather well, don't you think?' He winked at them and straightened himself up in his seat.

Ivy thought he was probably right. How long more would people be allowed to go on and on. A couple of people in their residence were pushing ninety this year. Most were well into their seventies and eighties.

Maggie laughed and talked over Ivy to Jack. 'You are right there, boy. People will be paying big money to have their birth certificates altered as soon as they reach sixty-five.'

She got a fit of laughing and Ivy had to laugh too. Maggie's laugh was infectious. Jack Other laughed along with them and then got a fit of coughing. Susie came along promptly with a bottle of water.

She always accompanied the residents to the Holy Redeemer church which most of them attended. Annie went to Christ Church, the Protestant church with the others.

When Jack recovered from his coughing fit, he remarked that all of them there had cheated the system before the system cheated them and they all laughed and agreed.

Vera walked slowly around the grounds and then sat and rested on a bench under the old weeping willow. It overlooked the small lake. She closed her eyes and listened. There was some birdsong nearby and it was calming. There was a gentle breeze that ruffled her hair. She got up after twenty minutes and decided that she would try and ring Judy now before dinner. She wondered whether she would be there.

She went to her room and lifted the phone and requested the number of her old home. It was answered after a few moments.

'Judy, it's Mum, how are you?'

A man's voice answered her. 'Judy is out at the minute, she should be back soon. Can I give her a message?'

'No, I will ring again shortly, thank you.'

Dismay flowed through her. He was already in the house! What was going on with her daughter?

She sank wearily onto her armchair. Sadness threatened to engulf her and a sense of helplessness too.

When Ivy arrived shortly with her paper, she found her friend looking profoundly down.

'Vera I've brought your paper. How do you feel now my dear?'

Vera sighed and thanked her friend. 'I've just learned since yesterday that my daughter has a new boyfriend and it is something I was not expecting, Ivy. I have no wish to keep anything from you. I know that you are no gossip.'

Ivy nodded. She knew nothing about Vera's family. Her grandson had visited yesterday, and she guessed that this is what caused her friend's sadness.

'Was it something your grandson said yesterday, to cause your upset, Vera?'

Vera nodded. 'Yes, the boys have just learned that their father wants a divorce and now suddenly there is another man in their lives. They are not happy, and neither am I Ivy, it is just not like my daughter at all.'

'Well Vera, all I can say is, just wait, things may not be as they seem. Your poor daughter is going through a bit of turmoil too, you know?'

Vera knew that very well. 'Thanks Ivy. It will sort itself out no doubt. I just worry about the boys and feel that I should be there still. In fact, if I were there, it probably would not have happened.'

As soon as she uttered those words, the thought struck her that it was precisely because she was not there, that it had happened. Her mind started turning somersaults.

Ivy stood up and looked at Vera. She realised the woman had not heard what she had said.

'Vera, come on to dinner, it's time. You will feel better when you have eaten, come on.'

After a dinner that she hardly tasted, Vera again went to her room and requested the same number. It rang for a while and then she heard the same male voice saying 'Hello'.

'May I please speak to Judy?' she asked quietly.

The person on the other end of the phone shouted 'Judy' at the top of his voice and a minute later her daughter came on the line.

She could tell that Judy was embarrassed.

'I just want to know what is happening in that house and your lives,' Vera said without preamble. 'I have had Charlie to visit and he is upset Judy. What is going on?'

'Mum, you mustn't worry. I wish I had seen you before Charlie. He is a pest, interfering like this. It was not the way you were supposed to hear the news.'

'What news, Judy? Your divorce is hardly through yet, is it? Now there is a new man for your children to contend with. Are you quite sane at this moment, do you think?'

'Mum, I know you won't understand. I have had no real companionship for years, as you well know. I have known Tommy a long time. I did not plan for all this to happen.'

As Judy took a breath, Vera said calmly. 'Yes I know you have been deprived of a male relationship since Michael went his own sweet way, but I am curious as to how and why I am now here, and your Tommy is now in residence, by the sound of it? To me, it sounds very well planned. Could you not have told me about him?'

'No Mum, it is nothing like that. It just happened, that's all. The boys will come around eventually I know.'

'You know Judy that Charlie is quite upset about the whole business and is worried about the twins' reaction? Could you not have waited for a better time, when your life was more organised?

'My life has never been organised Mum; it's chaotic from morning to night. I am stretched in all directions, please do not condemn me, you, my mother.'

Vera sighed, 'of course I will never condemn you Judy. You are my only daughter and I feel for all the difficulties you have in your life. I just hope that you have not added to them, love.'

'Look Mum, I will visit just as soon as possible, alright?'

Vera did not get any comfort from the phone conversation with Judy and felt even more alienated from her daughter and the life she had enjoyed for so many years.

Chapter 14

When Sylvie did not appear for Sunday dinner and then supper, Ivy was perturbed. She asked Annie if Sylvie had requested room service and was told that she had and had eaten both meals in her room. Annie thought it was a touch of arthritis that was bothering Sylvie. Seeing as how she had danced so vigorously on Friday night Ivy did not pass any comment. Later that night, she knocked at the door and hearing nothing, entered unbidden.

Her friend was lying in bed. The curtains were closed, and the light was off. Only the light from the bathroom was on. Ivy sat down in the chair beside the bed and stared at her best friend.

'He's been here, hasn't he? Has he hurt you, Sylvie?'

Sylvie did not answer. Her eyes were open, and she stared at the ceiling. Ivy took her friend's hand and spoke loudly. 'Sylvie, talk to me, tell me what's happened, please, I can't bear it when you are like this. You, of all people should know how I feel when someone is abused.' Despite not wanting to, she started to weep.

That seemed to galvanise Sylvie. 'Oh, stop crying Ivy, I don't like it when you cry. I'll be alright, it just takes a little time. And yes, he was here. His demands keep increasing. He knows too much about me and my family. He says I owe him. Seemingly my husband ruined him and his business. The bank foreclosed on him and he lost everything. Therefore, *I* owe him. Me, without anything Ivy, isn't that funny? The trouble is, he will tell everyone about my husband, and he will ruin my family. I am so proud that I was married to an important man. I cannot let him do that Ivy, I just cannot.'

Ivy had no answer to give her friend. She sat and digested this. 'But, Sylvie, it was the bank that foreclosed, not your husband, why can he not see that? I don't understand what he is so irate about. Banks do this to people every single day; that's what they do to survive and make a profit out of other people's misery and misfortune.'

Sylvie turned her head to Ivy and with tear-filled eyes said, 'that was not all Ivy. My husband also had an affair with Ken's wife, so now it's pay-back time.'

'But you don't believe him, surely? It's only his word and you have no way of proving if it is true. I would not believe a word that comes from that man's mouth.'

Sylvie shook her head and tears rolled down her cheeks. 'The trouble is, Ivy, it's true. I knew poor Brian had an eye for the ladies, you knew Brian Ivy. I confronted him once and he threatened to leave me. After that I was too scared.'

Ivy's mouth was dry, and she felt horror for her poor friend who had helped her so much, unbeknown to most people. It was so unfair and not to be borne.

Later when Sylvie had got a little calmer, Ivy left and crept along to her own room, where she sat staring straight ahead, her hands clenched tightly in her lap.

In her bedroom that night, Vera was wide awake and thinking of her family situation. Her sister was the only sibling left alive and was living miles away. Anyway, there was little she could do. She was crippled with arthritis and her husband looked after her. She was totally frustrated at her situation here; she was still able-bodied, was she not? Why could she not insist on moving back home? Then thinking of the strange Tommy in the house, she knew it was impossible. What about if she rented a place to live, near them? She thought about it and decided she would have a chat with the only person whom she knew would understand, Eva Wilson. She settled in bed a bit easier after making that decision.

On Monday morning, Vera enjoyed a back massage and it certainly made her feel a little more relaxed. While there, she overheard the two physios chatting as she got dressed.

'There is certainly a big improvement in most of our people's mobility, have you noticed?'

'Yes, it's amazing. I mentioned it to Eva last week. She is delighted. I can't think of what it is we are doing differently, can you?'

As they drifted off, Vera smiled to herself and thought of the way the old folks reacted to the dancing.

The Monday singsong was a bit subdued. Vera was not really in the mood for it. Maggie tried to inject some enthusiasm into the group.

'What about this choir we are supposed to have for Christmas? She asked this looking around at them all and making eye contact with them. Vera nodded and then made a big effort to respond to Maggie.

'Right you are, Maggie. Now is everyone sure we can do a proper carol-singing evening for the staff and any visitors that come. We will all have to pull together and maybe we can have some solos?'

Some of the oldies were quite at sea, it seemed. Ivy put up her hand and told everyone it was a great idea. She would volunteer for a solo and knew that she could do a duet with Jack Stroke, she also pointed out that Bob could play his drums and that would add something special.

Ken the Lech then suggested he would do a duet with Sylvie and grinned around at them all. Ivy turned to look at him and if looks could kill, he was gone.

Vera asked what the favourite carols might be and got an immediate and loud response. Maggie leaned back in her chair well pleased.

They then had a short but lively rendering of a few of the all-time favourites. By four o'clock, everyone streamed out of the room for afternoon tea, the mood had lightened considerably. Vera felt optimistic once more. She had an appointment to meet with Eva Wilson in the afternoon of Tuesday and wanted to write out exactly what she planned to say to her. She must be calm and articulate and not in any way upset, she knew that it all depended on how she came across to Eva. She knew that she was not like the poor dears who had dementia and were deteriorating. She had all her marbles and really was able to look after herself. If Eva knew why it was that she was moved here, she would naturally understand that this was not the place for Vera.

Vera was not to know that tonight's events would scupper her meeting with Eva and that their lives would be changed quite a lot afterwards.

On Tuesday morning, there was a lot of noisy rushing about heard before breakfast. People looking out of their bedroom doors on Vera's wing, saw medics rushing with a stretcher, heading towards the end of the corridor. Following them was the day nurse, Maura, looking flustered and red in the face. As she progressed down the corridor, she urged all the onlookers to go back into their bedrooms and stay there, until they were told to come out.

Vera went back inside her room. Honestly! They were being treated like children, told to stay in their rooms. What about breakfast? She checked her clock on her locker. Oh, it was only eight o'clock.

Breakfast would only be ready in another hour. What was happening, she wondered? Must be someone was sick she surmised, having seen the stretcher. She hoped it was not one of her favourite friends. She had not noticed who was outside in the corridor, it just seemed like a lot of people, staff were there too in their white uniforms. No doubt there would soon hear all about it.

At nine o'clock the bell for breakfast rang and doors immediately began opening and shuffling steps slowly headed to the dining room. Everyone was there and looking around anxiously. There was one place vacant

Chapter 15

The residents ate their breakfast in silence. All eyed the vacant chair from time to time. No one spoke out loud. There were a few whispers and then the usual deaf people asking: 'What's that?' loudly.

At the end of the meal when it appeared that all were finished, Miss Swift appeared looking serious and Maura stood beside her.

'My dear friends, I have a sad announcement to make today. We have lost a dear friend and companion, Ken Smith, who died sometime during the night. You will be glad to hear that he passed in his sleep and did not suffer. I know this will unsettle you all and if anyone needs to talk to Maura or myself or Mrs. Wilson, just let us know. We are here for you and we all feel the pain when someone passes.

Then they were all on their own. Little groups formed and heads wagged, and the general feeling was, it could have been any one of us. Life is uncertain. People drifted off then and the usual medication time came. There was no physio today as a mark of respect.

Most people drifted to the lounge after getting their medication. Vera sat in the usual place she picked, near to Jack Stroke. The daily newspapers were picked up, but nobody was reading them. Vera looked around and did not see any sad faces. She looked over at Jack.

'Well Jack, what do you make of that, eh? It was very sudden really, wasn't it? He seemed alright yesterday at the singsong, I thought.'

'Probably his heart Vera. The old codger thought he was a young fellow, quite the Lothario at times. That's the way of it, Vera, comes to us all. The only thing we are guaranteed in this life: death.' Jack started reading his paper.

Maggie piped up, 'just like Ivy and I were talking about on the bus on Sunday. She said we were all on the roundabout waiting for the last exit.'

There was some quiet laughter. 'A good analogy, I think,' said Mr. Burrow.

The one thing that nobody expressed, Vera noticed, was any kind of sadness or regret for the demise of Ken the Lech. She knew that she did not feel anything towards him except pity. He could have been a nice person if he wanted to. It seemed he never wanted to. There again, what do I know about his life? Maybe we are misjudging him. I am certainly guilty of that.

Ivy came into the room and went in to see the news on television. She loved the news and never missed it. She passed Vera and smiled warmly at her. There was no sign of Sylvie. She was the only one who seemed shocked at Miss Swift's announcement. Vera had seen her put her hands up to her mouth as the news came out of Miss Swift's mouth.

When all the residents were trooping into the dining room for dinner, Vera noticed some activity on her wing. There was activity in Ken's room, and she saw a man on a ladder at the end of the corridor doing something overhead. She imagined it was changing a light bulb that he was engaged in.

She decided to go and play the piano after dinner to calm her mind. She had been told that her appointment with Eva had been postponed due to the sudden death and that she could reschedule it.

She found Jack Stroke and Jack Other in a corner muttering away. She saw Jack Stroke's face and thought that he looked ill. Going up to them she asked them if they thought it would be insensitive to play the piano that day. Both men rose and shook their heads.

'Vera, go ahead girl, and play. Music is a great healer, some of the others may hear and come in.'

They both left the recreation room and Vera felt that she had interrupted something.

She did not stay for long. Her mood was not right for playing. She closed the piano and went to get a cup of tea. She found the two Jacks there again, huddled over the table at the window with Bob Grunt. She took her cup of tea and sat on the opposite side of the room. Ivy and Sylvie came in later with Maggie pushing a wheelchair of one of the most eager 'dancers'. They joined her and she was glad to have someone to chat to. Sylvie looked brighter and Ivy was positively glowing. Nobody mentioned the death at all.

'What is going on in our wing, does anyone know?' asked Vera.

They all shook their heads and wondered how long it would be before another person would fill Ken's place.

'Will we able to have our dance this Friday?' wondered Maisie in the wheelchair, 'I so look forward to it.'

'We better wait and see how quickly things return to normal, I imagine', said Ivy, matter-of-factly. She then caught sight of the men huddled at the far side of room and a frown came to her face.

'Excuse me ladies for just a moment, will you?'

They watched as Ivy crossed over to the men. She bent and whispered something in Jack Stroke's ear, and he shook his head. It seemed to Vera that Ivy walked back to the table with a lighter tread.

After supper that night, Mrs. Eva Watson WILSON appeared in the dining room. Everyone fell silent wondering what she was there for. It was unusual.

She started by again sympathising with their loss. However, it seemed that the doctor needed to know what exactly happened Ken Smith as he had been in good enough health. There would be someone in the nurse's office and people were encouraged to drop in and chat about Ken privately, and maybe some light would be shed on any problems the man had or if anyone had heard anything that night. She stressed that everyone was of course upset and that was another reason why it might be good to talk about it to someone. If they did not feel comfortable talking to a stranger, she would be available herself in Miss Swift's office for the rest of the evening. She smiled around at them all and then bid them goodnight.

They all looked at each other and wondered what she meant. They could hardly tell her that he had a great time dancing on Friday night, and he was fine then, and at the singsong. Some of the old dears who were suffering from dementia were at sea about the whole thing and did not really understand what all the fuss was about.

Jack Stroke and Jack Other decided that someone should make the effort to say something, and each went to talk to Eva. As far as they were concerned Ken was fine and they did not notice anything. It was in Eva Wilson's presence that they learned from her that Ken had a head injury which was unexplained. She did muse that he could easily have fallen out of bed and hit his head on his locker. Jack Stroke was puzzled. Ken was steady on his feet and did not suffer the normal stiffness and slowness that most of them suffered from. Jack Other later asked Jack Stroke if he thought that Ken could have had some alcohol taken. It was not unheard of. They did not mention this to Eva Wilson though. As far as Eva was concerned, alcohol was forbidden, and she assumed everyone abided by that rule. They were not going to be the ones to enlighten her.

Chapter 16

There was a small memorial service in the recreation room a few days later and all the residents and staff attended. A clergyman and a clergywoman of different denominations spoke and prayed for the dead man. Afterwards there were some special refreshments in the dining room and people circulated freely.

'Is there going to be a singsong, now?' enquired one old dear who did not really know what was going on. Miss Swift hastened to explain that there would be no singsong today out of respect for Ken.

'Oh, that's sad. I really love to dance, you know.'

Miss Swift looked puzzled but then smiled indulgently at the old lady. Some of the others who were nearby nearly dropped their teacups in fright.

They all drifted away gradually and went to the lounge or garden.

Vera and Maggie sat in the fading evening sunshine beside the lake and pondered the events. The two Jacks had confided the news to them that Ken had an unexplained head injury.

Susie passed by pushing Bob Grunt and he asked to be left beside the two women for a while. Susie said that she would come by in fifteen minutes to push him back.

'Well Bob! What do you think of all this business?' Vera asked the man who was usually so non-communicative.

'It's like this, ladies; I for one, am not a bit sad. He has been a thorn in my side for as long as I can remember.'

Vera looked at him sharply. 'Why Bob? I thought you got on well with him generally. I have never heard you say a bad word about anyone here.'

Bob just grunted and then muttered, 'I have my reasons, believe me, but enough about him, what I want to know is, will it affect our Friday night specials?'

Vera was startled by his candour and obvious distaste of the dead man. Maggie giggled and told him not to worry. All would resume presently and not to worry.

Jack Other next appeared and approached the bench where the women were seated. When Maggie repeated Bob's worry about Friday nights, Jack shook his head.

'Might be a bit of trouble there. Jack Stroke forgot to push the CCTV camera back to the right position after the dance and they have discovered it. Now they are doing a right job on it and it may not be possible to move it again, so we're scuppered, if that is the case.

Vera had not realised that there was a CCTV camera on their wing at all. She knew there were

102

some in the grounds and outside the entrance and back exit area. Now she guessed that the huddle of men she had witnessed had probably been discussing this and how to disarm it.

'How did they disarm it then, Jack?' she asked.

'No problem, a chair and walking stick. It is only on for part of the day anyway. We found that out from Sid a while back. We were able to distract the office staff during tea break and push the camera to face the ceiling, no problem to us experts.' Jack grinned proudly.

'So, the camera has been like that all this time?' Maggie asked.

'Ah no. Generally, we remember to reverse the procedure after the dance-night. This time Jack forgot. I told him he must be starting that Alzheimer thing!'

Vera and Maggie looked at each other. They realised that there was no record of them going back to their rooms but also that there was no record of anyone going to Ken's room that Monday night.

'I wonder if the authorities suspect that Ken might have had a fight with someone, otherwise why would they want to talk to us about events that night?' Maggie was a shrewd woman and a step ahead of the others.

Vera thought about her own confrontation with the dead man, and that set up another chain of thought.

The daylight was definitely receding now, and Susie appeared, to push Bob back. The others all rose to their feet and started slowly walking back to the house.

Vera walking beside Bob, remarked to Susie that it was unusual to see her there in the evenings.

'Sometimes I get the chance to do extra duty, Vera. Sid is out sick since yesterday, so I was asked. It is a good opportunity for me to make some extra money, you know.

Vera who was aware how hard the Filipinos worked in this country asked about her family. It was as she expected. Susie came from a big family and had come over to live with a sister who had come here some years earlier. Every spare cent they earned, was sent back home for the education and health care of the rest of the family. Her sister was a nurse in the nearby hospital. Susie also hoped to train one day as a nurse, when she felt her English was proficient enough.

The lounge was full of residents, but talk was subdued. Maggie looked around at everyone there and noted the long faces.

'What is up with all of you? You look as if you've lost your wits, all of you! We will rally, my friends, and will find a way of having our mad evenings again, I promise.' She knew that it was the Friday evenings that had them looking so glum, not poor Ken's demise. There was a sudden lifting up of faces and a glimmer of hope showed on them all.

Jack Stroke asked her how they could circumvent the CCTV. Maggie shook her head.

'That is up to you clever boys, I don't understand the damn things. With all your expertise and cunning, I am certain that you will find a way for us.'

There was renewed chatter and things looked a lot better, they thought. Mr. Burrow suddenly stood up and appearing rather excited, he told them that his nephew and his son had a security business and if anyone could help, it was them. He got a round of applause after that announcement and the two Jacks went over and sat on either side of him.

For the next few days, the three men could be seen walking in the grounds, all busy talking and arguing vigorously.

Life settled into the usual routine and the residents had the physio exercises to look forward to. The two physios had added to Maggie's tape of Abba and knew the old people reacted with much more enthusiasm to the lively music.

One morning after their exercises they all went for their morning coffee or tea and Vera encountered Susie emerging from Miss Swift's office. The girl was mopping her eyes and looked distressed.

She did not see Vera as she went to pass, and Vera called her. 'Susie dear, whatever is the matter? Can I help you at all?'

Susie met Vera's eye and shook her head. 'I'm sorry Vera, it is nothing really. Nothing that I can trouble you about.'

Vera took the girl's arm and walked towards the door to the gardens. 'Come on, Susie, a trouble shared is a trouble halved, as they say.'

As Susie looked at her enquiringly, Vera shook her head. 'Never mind the meaning, girl. Come out to the garden with me now.'

They walked into the rose garden and Vera pointed to a bench under a tree. They both sat and Vera waited. She would not push the girl for her problem to be told.

After a few more sobs, the girl finally calmed. The story then came out in bits and pieces. Vera knew she would have to be patient and not ask questions until Susie had finished.

She had been seen coming out of Ken's room and had been reported. Miss Swift had questioned her about her presence in his room and had been very hostile towards her. She told the girl that her job here was at stake and she would not be given a reference on leaving. That seemed to be the story in its entirety. Vera waited for more, but the girl was now silent.

Vera asked gently, 'who reported you, Susie?'

'It was Sid, Vera. I was in Ken's room it was true, only once and I am not a thief.'

'I believe you Susie, of course you are not a thief. Can you tell me why you were in Ken's room?'

'It is so embarrassing Vera, I am ashamed. I could not tell Miss Swift about it, but I can tell you. Mr. Ken, he is always smiling at me and asked me two weeks ago to get something from his room. When I went there, he followed me in. He wanted me to do something dishonourable Vera, and I refused. He grabbed me and tried to stop me leaving the room. I was very scared. He is so strong…..sorry, was strong.' She cried again.

Vera could understand this story completely and believed the poor little girl. She spoke quietly to Susie and told her that a lot of women there had the same problem with Ken, he was well known for it. She asked Susie how she managed to extricate herself from the room.

'I did something dishonourable too Vera, I kicked him in his leg and ran from the room.'

She looked at Vera as though expecting disapproval and was surprised to see Vera smiling.

'Good for you Susie. He needed that and he asked for it. What a horrible man.'

Susie nodded and said, 'yes he offered me money to do this bad thing and it was a lot of money, Vera. He said I could help my family a lot with it and that he would pay me every time I came to his room.' She shook her head vigorously and her hair swung out and off her shoulders. 'He thought I was one of those women, Vera.' Now the girl was feeling angry and Vera was happy about that. She should feel offended and angry.

'Now Miss Swift, she thinks that I am unreliable because Sid told her. I might be asked to leave here, and I do not know how I will manage to find another job, like the one in this place. Here people are nice to me and I am very happy.'

Vera said nothing but thought for a few minutes.

'Susie, I understand what has happened and I don't think that Miss Swift has. Do you mind if I have a word with her? I too had a problem with Ken.'

'You too?' Poor Susie looked dumbfounded.

Vera felt like saying to her, yes, even us oldies were fair game for the old lecher. She just smiled at the girl and patted her hand.

'Leave it to me Susie and do not worry any more about it.'

They walked slowly back towards the house.

Vera decided to tackle the problem at once and knocked and entered Miss Swift's office. She was not there, and Vera felt dismayed. When your adrenaline is flowing is the best time to attack, she thought.

Her secretary told her that Miss Swift had to go and speak with some people at the police station and would be back after dinner.

Vera felt alarmed. The police station! Was it about Ken and about Susie being accused of being in his room? As she went into the lounge to rest before dinner, she realised that she had not thought about Judy's situation at all since Ken died. What was wrong with her?

Chapter 17

Summer gradually came to an end. The trees began to shed their leaves and the grounds of Rosebank House were covered in gold and orange carpets That too was beautiful, Vera and her friends thought. The singsongs continued but the Friday dances had not resumed since Ken's death. Mr. Burrow was waiting for information from his nephew. The singsongs were turning more towards Christmas carols and they were getting word perfect now and there was a bit of harmony emerging from some of the singers. The two Jacks had lovely bass voices and Mr. Burrow was a passable tenor. Maggie switched from alto to soprano regularly without noticing. Sylvie and Ivy were remarkably good sopranos.

Miss Swift announced one day after dinner that there was a special treat in store for them. A local artist was willing to come and give an art class one afternoon a week. Everyone must have a go, Miss Swift insisted, and inexperience was not an excuse. She padded off happily after this declaration.

They all looked at each other in surprise.

'I cannot draw a straight line,' complained Bob Grunt 'and she expects us to sit through a couple of hours of that?'

Vera chuckled. 'Straight lines don't come into it, Bob, it's just about spreading a bit of paint about and seeing what it looks like.'

'It will be great fun I think,' Ivy put in.

Maggie recalled the craft classes they had endured before Vera came. 'There were so many accidents with people stabbing themselves with needles, they had to stop it hurriedly.'

'Do you remember poor Maisie with her embroidery on her knee? Then to discover she had stitched it to her trousers!'

There was a lot of laughter at that.

'Yes, and Ken used a needle as a toothpick at one session and there was blood all over the place. He looked like Dracula!'

They drifted off for their siesta and Vera to her piano. She had been in touch with Judy and been assured by her that Tommy was not a permanent feature in the house; just now and then to hold the fort while she was at work. Vera was not reassured at all by this. Charlie had started school now and she was looking forward to hearing about how he was settling in. She had written him a letter and hoped he would start corresponding with her. It might help the lad.

She left her practice and went to get some tea and saw Mr. Burrow having afternoon tea with a visitor. She wondered if it were his nephew and hoped something could be arranged. She had thought of going to Eva Wilson to request permission to have the dances regularly, but the others were adamant that she would not allow it. It was the insurance risk that had them all terrified.

The business with Ken had nearly faded from their memories by now and they heard nothing more about his death, so it must have been a sad accident, they assumed.

Sylvie had become her usual domineering self again and reigned like a queen in the lounge at nights. Vera did not mind playing bridge with her, she was a good player and most of the time the players enjoyed it. Even Ivy had come out of her shell a bit more, Vera thought.

Mr. Burrow had an announcement tonight and everyone paid close attention. He told them he had spoken to his nephew and there was a way around the CCTV but it required precision and care. Most of the residents hadn't a clue of what he was speaking about and Vera certainly didn't. She looked around and saw Maggie nod knowingly and the men also. She hoped they understood and that they could start plotting their next 'naughty' night.

Everyone shuffled off to bed in a more optimistic frame of mind.

Susie was a happy girl since Vera spoke with Miss Swift. It took a quite a bit of explaining and afterwards Miss Swift called Susie in to the office and apologised. She also spoke to Sid the Snake and asked him about his motives in reporting Susie, since there was no money stolen as far as the authorities were concerned. That put him in his place and since then, he had avoided Susie.

Vera was suspicious of him however and wondered why it was money, he had mentioned to Miss Swift. She decided she would be more observant and keep an eye open all the time.

At the end of the week, one evening, there was a new resident. He came in for supper with Mrs. Wilson and was introduced as Mr. Power: Duncan Power. Vera was sitting next to him and introduced herself and Maggie who sat opposite.

'Don't worry Duncan, you will get to know everyone soon. I have not been here long, and I can tell you that it's a very friendly place.'

'Eh?' queried Duncan, his head on one side.

'Oh Lord, he's Mutt and Jeff,' muttered Maggie. She leaned in, and repeated loudly, 'We are all friendly here, Duncan, you are gonna have a ball.'

Jack Other snorted and turned it into a cough. Talk resumed as normal and Vera tried to include Duncan, but it was obvious that the poor man was very deaf.

They all retired to the lounge and Vera and Maggie took control of Duncan and brought him along too. He was quite slow compared to them but agreed with everything they suggested. He sat beside Maggie and Ivy and they tried to find out what he was interested in. It seemed he liked cards and played bridge. Sylvie heard and was delighted.

'New blood, how wonderful,' she gushed. 'Would you care to have a game tonight, Duncan?'

'Eh?' Duncan looked from Ivy to Maggie to Sylvie.

After a lot of explaining, Duncan agreed to play with Sylvie. Maggie said, sotto voce, that she was DEFinitely exhausted from all the explaining and was off to bed.

Vera and Ivy wondered how the game would proceed and they partnered each other nervously. They need not have worried. Once the cards were dealt, Duncan blossomed. Sylvie, to give her credit, raised her voice considerably and made sure he understood her bids. She probably would have got through to him anyway with the booming voice she was blessed with. Duncan looked much more relaxed and at home.

The next morning after breakfast as he met with Susie and she explained the week's routine, Vera dropped over and whispered, 'try to get him fixed up with a hearing aid, will you Susie?'

Art classes commenced that week and most of the residents gave it a try. Most of the ladies loved it, a few of the men were keen, but not all. The artist, Paul, was very patient and kind and helpful too. He led them along gradually and suggested they try different media to find out which type suited them. They all tried pastels and watercolours that day, and most were pleased with their efforts. They were surprised that two hours passed so quickly.

Ivy was thrilled with the class and showed real talent. Sylvie was not so thrilled with her efforts and Ivy encouraged her to be patient. It was after all their first lesson.

Susie was with them for the lesson and took part as well. She told Vera that she had always wanted to do art but never had the chance. She soaked up every tip Paul gave them and at the end of the lesson had a reasonable pastel of the items he had laid out on the table. He looked at everyone's work and gave his thoughts on how they were managing. He spent most time with Ivy and Susie and seemed impressed with their paintings. Poor Duncan gave up almost at once. He threw the pastel down and muttered angrily. Vera went over and tried to get him to start again.

'I did not come here to do art,' he shouted, quite loudly, 'I left school a long time ago, you know!'

Maggie came over and put her arm around his shoulder. 'I know, Duncan lad, it helps to pass the time, and the more variety we have, the better for our brains. We don't want to stagnate, now do we?'

'I would like to be left to stagnate Mag...Maggie.' Vera thought that she would ask Susie about his background. It would help to know more about him, but before she had a chance, Maggie and Mr. Burrow appeared in the lounge that night looking flushed and excited. They were ready for their usual Friday night again.

Chapter 18

The two Jacks and Mr. Burrow were constantly meeting at every opportunity to finalise the complicated steps they had to follow to change the CCTV for the night in question. It involved one going to the office and turning off the cameras on the bedroom wings and rewinding the machine to four o'clock the previous morning, the quietest time in the day, just before heading down to the recreation room. Whoever was on duty that night had to be distracted for ten minutes and away from the office area. The procedure had to be reversed after the dance finished.

It was decided not to include Duncan in the proceedings as he was too new to the house and would be totally at sea. Maybe when he had been there for some time and they all knew him better. He was also going to get two hearing aids in the coming days. He had already had a couple of outings to town to the local optical centre, which also provided hearing aids.

That September afternoon was sunny and balmy, and Maggie and Vera had a stroll around the gardens after their siesta. They were quietly excited about the coming night activities but nervous too. It all depended on the swiftness and precision of the men involved. Maggie was going to be the main distraction and went over her act again and again with Vera.

At supper there was an air of quiet suspense and nobody was quite relaxed. They all managed to eat their supper and conversation was careful if subdued. They all trooped off to the lounge as normal and some watched television or played cards. Dennis was anxious for a game of bridge and Mr. Burrow agreed to partner him against Sylvie and Vera.

Jack Stroke walked up to the dining room at regular intervals, getting a cup of tea each time and observing what was going on in the office. In the staff room he could see the playing cards on the small table where they would sit later. They would leave the office area when they went for their dinner in the staff room around eleven. That is where their coffee would be 'doctored'.

He felt a bit nervous about doing this. He, like all the residents loved these evenings and knew that if they were discovered Mrs. Wilson would be livid and the restrictions imposed would be immediate. He knew in his heart that the morale and wellbeing of the residents had improved immensely since Vera had come into the house and did not want to see that end.

At last the hour came for them all to gradually leave and go to their rooms. The last to go as usual were Maggie and Jack Stroke. As they parted, Jack gave Maggie the thumbs up sign.

Silence descended. Mano and Sid did their usual rounds, bringing carafes of water to some rooms and helping the three wheelchair cases into bed. It seemed to be busier than ever tonight, they thought. Everyone requested something; water here; help with a radiator there; finding a book which had slipped under the bed; searching for the purse that had definitely been left on the locker: that took a bit of time and then it was found in the bathroom cabinet: 'Of course, I forgot that is where I left it!'

By the time eleven o'clock came, they were more than ready for their dinner. They had just sat down to a lovely curry when they were interrupted by Maggie. She was in a state. She left her glasses in the lounge and now could not find them. Please could they help? She was lost without them. Maggie was a drama queen and indeed had done a lot of amateur acting in her youth.

Sid sighed. 'Can we just have our dinner first, Maggie?'

'Oh, it'll just take a minute, I just can't reach behind the sofa where I had them, please boys, if the two of you just pull out the sofa I can squeeze in and get them.' She put on her most dramatic face and the men thought she was about to burst into tears.

Hurriedly they got to their feet. Maggie slowly began her procession to the lounge, taking as long as possible. They entered the lounge and put on the lights. Maggie pointed to the sofa on the near wall and they pulled it out. Sid went behind and searched.

'Can't see nothin' here,' he commented.

'Wait, it's still too dark Sid. Mano, will you put on the other table lights?'

Mano complied and more searching went on. Sid was muttering angrily at this stage.

'Wait, I actually think it might have been the other sofa, Sid.'

The two men went to the far wall and pulled out that sofa. Sid went behind and searched, and Mano felt down behind all the cushions.

'Maggie, are you quite sure you left them here?'

'I know I did, Sid. They are certainly here, I'm sure.'

The men straightened up and pushed back the sofa. Maggie glanced at the clock on the wall and relaxed.

'Mano would you just check that big armchair in the television room, I've just remembered I watched the news. The two men went into the small room off the lounge and Maggie again checked the clock.

'Found them!'

Mano and Sid emerged from the room, Mano holding the missing glasses. Mano was beaming and Sid was looking less than pleased.

'Mano, you angel you! I am so grateful. I will have to let Mrs. Wilson know how wonderful you men are.'

She smiled happily. 'Now enjoy your meal, you deserve it.'

As the men switched off the table lamps and main lights, Maggie walked very slowly towards her wing, the men coming behind had to adjust their pace too.

'Now we will have to reheat the food in the microwave, it's gone cold. What an old bag!' Sid was put out. It was the busiest night they had for ages. He meant to win back all the money he had lost to Mano over the past week.

At midnight, the procession began and all trooped to the recreation room as before. They waited for about five minutes to see if there was any movement from the staff room or office. Not a sound. As usual the music began quietly but quickly became louder and livelier as the time passed.

Everyone was in their element and Vera glanced up now and again from the piano and watched the rapt faces; that sight was enough to put joy in anyone's heart, she thought. Bob tapped happily away on his drums, in between moving around in his wheelchair to the music.

Again, it was Sylvie who requested the craziest music. 'Oh Vera, do you know the Hucklebuck?'

This was an old favourite of most of their age group and brought back memories of their youth and the big showbands.

As she belted out the tune, many started singing as well as dancing and Sylvie went wild. Ivy could not keep up with her at all. Jack Stroke got a bit worried and went over to Sylvie. 'Better not overdo it girl, just remember your age.'

'Don't worry about me Jack. Jealousy will get you nowhere.'

After that Vera calmed them down with some old-time waltzes. She was feeling wrecked herself. How did they keep going, she wondered?

As she walked back to her bedroom, she wondered why they were there at all. Music brought them all alive she knew. Then she thought about their mental capacity and hers. Alright, there were some who were slipping, but generally, they were all marvellous for their age.

Jack and Mr. Burrows now had a difficult job. They just hoped the two men were dozing in the staff room as the office had no comfortable chairs to doze in. Jack paused outside the office and gently opened the door. Nobody was inside thankfully. They must be in the staff room. No sound emerged from there either. He was back out and heading to bed in five minutes. Mr. Burrows was keeping watch and when Jack came back out, they quickly disappeared onto their wing. It was set to start recording again at four o'clock this morning and now it was only two-thirty.

The dancers were all exhausted and drank the water they had been provided with earlier. Some took a sleeping tablet and others felt no need of one.

Sylvie slept like a baby and Ivy too had the best sleep of her life. Vera shook out the remaining drops of her whiskey and decided she would ring Judy again and request a visit.

Chapter 19

By nine thirty-five, a few people made their way to the dining room for breakfast, among them was Vera, who was starving. She had slept well but her wrists and hands were aching. She knew the cause and wondered if there were any sore feet.

Susie and Annie were on duty this morning. After tapping on the doors of the people who might need help and told go away, they sat in the dining room and wondered if they should alert the nurse to their absence. Vera overheard them and was alarmed.

'Girls, it is Saturday, after all. Have you never had a lie in on a Saturday? It's only heaven after the weekly routine. Tomorrow it'll be all fuss and feathers as usual.'

The girls agreed with her. Susie confided, 'it's just since Ken was found that we need to be on our toes, Vera. We got an awful shock, you know. Nobody was expecting it.'

Vera knew that. When anyone was seriously ill, they were usually moved to the big house where there was a sick bay. It was thought that if people were on the way out, it would be unsettling for the other residents to witness. Nobody had died on either wing for as long as the staff could remember.

Annie lowered her voice and whispered that the police had wanted an investigation into his sudden death as the postmortem examination was 'inconclusive', whatever that means, she said.

Vera was shocked again. 'I thought he fell out of bed or hit his head somehow on his locker?'

'Well, we were all told not to discuss it between ourselves. "The authorities know what they are doing", we were told.'

Annie looked around the room and smiled. 'Honestly how else could it have happened. He was in his seventies for heaven's sake. If he did not fall, what do they think happened? That one of the others bonked him on the head with his hot water bottle?'

The two girls started to giggle, and Vera smiled with them. Sadly, she realised that as far as these young girls were concerned, the over seventies were too over the hill for any life at all. When did she come to the realisation that age did not matter in the slightest? Probably only when she became less busy in her life. When was that? On retirement or widowhood? She could not remember now. It's how you feel inside, she believed. Some people, she felt, would never feel old, and on the other hand, some would never feel young. Such a paradox. In particular, she remembered a young girl who worked in the office that she had worked in for a while. The girl was twenty-one and the bookkeeper in the firm. She had married a man twice her age and whether it was because of that, she was regarded as middle-aged and never mixed with the younger girls in the office. She dressed and spoke like a staid, middle-aged woman. Vera wondered what happened to her in later life.

She became aware of the girls talking and Susie in particular, about the art class. It seemed that Susie was smitten and could not wait for the next session. If she was not on duty, she was going to come in and attend anyway, she said. Annie offered to change duty with her if she was on that day and Susie thanked her.

Susie then rose to go and talk to Duncan who was sitting by himself. He looked fresh and energetic compared to the rest of the diners.

Vera left and went to her room and requested an outside line to call her daughter. She was relieved to be answered by Judy. They chatted about the boys and Judy said that Charlie was settling in well and liked it so far. Vera did not want to ask about Tommy if she could help it. Instead she asked if were possible to bring some whiskey the next visit. Judy promised that she would and thought that she would be free next Saturday or Sunday. Vera asked if she would bring the twins also. She really missed the busy household now. At first, she had not really been lonely for them as she was settling in, but now that she was used to the routine and had made lots of friends, she really missed the boys and their noisy energy. She was going to broach the subject of her returning to live with Judy, after all she was only here temporarily Judy had said. She did not know how she would react if Judy showed a reluctance to have her back. She would know then that it had been planned. Well, she would cross that bridge when she came to it.

After supper that night, Miss Swift announced that there would be the annual outing the next day, depending on the weather of course. There was a large outdoor concert going to take place in the town park. Most of the schools were taking part and the local brass band. If any person did not feel like going, or felt ill, they should let her know. A large coach had been booked to take them all comfortably. All staff were coming plus some volunteers from the community.

In the lounge later, this was the main topic of conversation and even though most of them were tired after the Friday night dancing, there was still a frisson of excitement in the air. Both Ivy and Maggie were all for it and appeared not to be tired at all. Vera did not know whether she would have recovered sufficiently for it and decided to wait until the morning to see how she felt.

Everyone was out of the lounge and in bed by nine that night. The weekend staff were in and looking forward to a quiet night. After the residents were settled, they tidied up the lounge and recreation room and that was basically all they had to do, unless someone called them from their room, which rarely happened. Now and again one of them might have to go across to the big house and help out in the sick bay, but there were only two long term residents there for the past six months. They were both bedridden and not compos mentis and needed frequent medication and turning in bed.

The local population regarded employment at Rosebank as a much sought-after position; staff were treated fairly, and it was believed that the residents were extremely well cared for and fortunate people.

Mrs. Wilson was highly regarded by the locals too. She had looked after her sick husband for many years, gradually accepting a couple of sick or ailing friends to stay in the house as well. When he finally died, she was asked by the mayor of the town if she would consider opening a retirement home in her spacious house. After consideration, she decided that is what she would do. For several years, the big house was the residential home. Then as time passed, she realised that the old house was not that suitable and to make it more amenable for mobile people, would cost too much, so the idea of the modern building came into being. Local funding and a Government grant helped to bring it all to fruition. Now it was the place where many people would aspire to retire to, but numbers were restricted to what the new building could accommodate, namely, sixteen places.

Chapter 20

There were fewer people than normal people in the minibus going to church. Maggie, Ivy and Vera were there as were the two Jacks and a couple of the wheelchairs, Maisie being one. Duncan was there too which they thought surprising, as he was quite a strong willed and noisy agitator at times. He had shown his will at the art class first and many times after. He wanted the tv up to its highest level of course and that took some sorting out. He was faddy about his food and complained loudly if all was not to his satisfaction. The others were surprised at all this, as he came across first as a most quiet and amiable fellow. The only time he was perfectly peaceful, was playing bridge. He was going to get hearing aids fitted during the week and they wondered how he would adapt to sound.

Vera decided after church and buying her paper that she would after all, attend the concert. She would then have the crosswords to look forward to afterwards.

They were like a lot of excited schoolchildren as they boarded the coach after dinner. It was an overcast day but not cold. Many of the women brought woolen shawls, just in case. They chattered all the way to the park. Then it was time to form into lines, two by two and the wheelchairs were organised by the staff. Vera found herself walking beside Mr.

Burrow. Ivy and Sylvie were together of course. They were led to the area, which was allocated to them, not too close to the bandstand, but off to the side, surrounded by flower beds of chrysanthemums and wallflowers. The seating arrangement was well thought out. The nearby toilets were within easy reach too.

They all settled and waited for the music to begin, looking around at all the different bands in their varied uniforms. The air was full of happy anticipation.

Then it was on, full blast and the friends from Rosebank started tapping their feel and nodding to the lively beat. It was all modern music, and the oldies were delighted. It was not long before an ear-blasting version of music from Mamma Mia soon had them up on their feet. Sylvie and Ivy were gyrating on the grass at the edge of their section. They were totally oblivious of the smiles and nudges of other people. Jack Stroke held onto Maisie's chair and wheeled her forward and back much to her delight as she clapped her hands over her head. Vera was dancing with Mr. Burrow. Most of the others found someone to dance with. After some time, the staff became aware of what was happening. They looked at each other and wondered if they should stop them, but Mrs. Wilson, also present, shook her head at them. It was obvious to all the staff that the residents were letting their hair down and really getting into the spirit of the music. Soon everyone was clapping, and many others were dancing on the grass where there was room. There was much applause when the selection of music finished. Then the dancers sat down and got their breath back. The brass band was next, and the residents took advantage of the more serious music to have a cold drink, given out by the staff and have a snack to eat. They could hardly wait for the lively music to start again. The concert lasted three hours and the residents of Rosebank House enjoyed every single moment. They were glad of the breaks provided by the brass band section but otherwise were nearly all on the grass bopping and moving as energetically as they were capable of.

Finally, it was over, and there was a rush to the toilets before boarding the coach again. Vera was in early and as she washed her hands got a tap on the shoulder Turning around, she saw a familiar face but could not put a name on in.

'It's Vera Crosbie, isn't it?' A fair-haired woman looked at her keenly. 'Don't you remember me? Molly Burke? We worked together in that charity shop for a couple of years, just after you retired, remember?'

Of course, she could. Now she remembered the jolly woman who was always laughing and cracking jokes at the charity shop.

'Of course, I do. I have not seen you in years, Molly. How are you?'

'It's been years since we met, and I have always wondered how you were. I did so want to meet you, especially in recent months, to have a serious chat.'

'Oh, really?'

'Yes Vera, my heart has been broken these past few years and then when I heard about Judy, I just wanted to meet you, but did not know where you had moved to.'

Vera looked at her sharply. 'What about Judy, Molly?'

Molly looked around at the throng in the toilet area, people queuing and trying to get to the wash hand basins.

'Look, could we go outside Vera?'

Outside the toilet block was a longer queue. Molly looked around and asked Vera if they could nip across the road to that coffee shop and have a cup of coffee or tea.

Vera was so interested in what Molly had to say that she did not hesitate for a moment. 'Come on, let's go.'

Over coffee in the quiet café, Molly told Vera her story and Vera listened, her heart beating faster as she recounted her sorry story.

Her daughter had an unhappy marriage, but worse, an abusive marriage and in the end, the husband served time in prison for assaulting her. There was a barring order against him, although for a time that did not stop him from trying to get back into the house. He often threatened to kill her and the kids. They had two children who were terrified of him.

Vera shook her head and sympathised with Molly.

'Wait, you have not heard the end of it, Vera.' She put her hand on Vera's arm. 'A couple of months ago my daughter heard on the grapevine that Tommy had taken up with another woman. When she said her name, I immediately thought of you; I knew you had a daughter called Judy. I got my daughter to inquire if it was your daughter and found out that it is. I am so upset and worried, Vera. I wonder if she knows the sort of man that Tommy is?'

As soon as Vera had heard the name Tommy her heart had plummeted. She had no doubt that this was the man her daughter was involved with.

'He was involved with drugs and alcohol abuse, Vera, and was supposed to go on rehabilitation courses, both for the drugs and alcohol abuse and for anger control. The reason he was released early was because he attended these courses. He only served a couple of months of his sentence because he attended the courses.'

'Is he off drugs and everything now, do you know Molly?'

Molly sighed and shook her head. 'My daughter does not think so. She has a Social Welfare officer who is a friend who visits her often and she says that Tommy is frequenting the same bars and clubs and is hanging around with the same rabble of losers still.'

Vera put her head in her hands. 'Oh, the poor boys. Charlie was right after all. He told me that he was not a nice person.'

They discussed the problem further and Molly wondered if it would be wise to warn Judy, as he might erupt if confronted by her, and she had seen what he inflicted on her daughter, who had been hospitalised. She wondered if it might be better to tell one of her friends, or maybe someone she worked with.

Vera did not know the answer to that and told Molly she would have to go and think deeply about it. She was so thankful for being told the truth and appreciated Molly telling her.

'After all, you could have just said nothing to me and instead, you had to tell me about your daughter's private life, which was not easy.'

They embraced and parted. Molly gave her the phone number at work, where she could be reached and promised to help in any way that she could.

Vera started walking and her head was in a whirl. Would Judy listen to her and if not, who could intervene? She never felt so desperate in her life, and angry too. How can someone who has hurt his wife be allowed out of prison so quickly. It was so unfair. What if he started to illtreat the boys? Would Judy be strong enough to go and seek help?

Chapter 21

It was only when the bus pulled into Rosebank that Vera was discovered missing. Ivy remembered seeing her coming from the toilets, as she was in the queue. But she did not see her after that.

Mrs. Wilson, who travelled back in her car was contacted and there was a lot of coming and going. They thought she might have alighted in the first batch of people and gone to her room. Everyone was busy with the people who were less mobile and the wheelchairs, and all in all they were all feeling tired, so concentration was at a low ebb.

Susie did not feel too worried. She knew that Vera was mentally alert and 'all there', as did Maggie and the two Jacks. Still, it began to worry them when there was no trace found of her in the house.

Finally, the police were notified, and got details of the missing woman from Miss Swift and Mrs. Wilson. Then Susie and Mrs. Wilson drove back the way they had come and went back into the park and scanned the area. The police car drove slowly all along the nearby streets.

Vera was found thirty minutes later, sitting at a bus stop. When Eva Wilson approached Vera, the woman looked at her blankly.

'Are you alright, Vera?' Mrs. Wilson sat down beside Vera and looked keenly at her.

After a couple of seconds of staring ahead, Vera turned to Eva, 'Oh Eva---sorry, Mrs. Wilson. I have had such a bad shock that I cannot think straight. I thought that if I could get a bus to my daughter's house, I could help her. Now, I don't think it's a good idea and the coach is gone back to Rosebank.'

Mrs. Wilson was not too perturbed but just a little alarmed. It was obvious that Vera knew her and associated her with Rosebank; she had realised that the coach was gone, so what sort of shock could have momentarily deranged this elderly woman. Now was not the time to question Vera. Instead she took her hand.

'Susie and I have come looking for you and now we will bring you back, Vera.'

Vera got up and allowed herself to be led to Eva's car. Eva then went over to the police car and spoke with the driver.

Back at the house, nobody seemed to have noticed Vera's return except Jack Stroke. He was in the foyer when Vera returned. All the others were in the lounge except those who had decided to go to bed early. Susie brought her to her room and then asked if she had eaten. Vera shook her head and said that she was not hungry but would like a cup of tea. No, she said, she did not want to go to the lounge, she wanted to go to bed after her cup of tea. Susie told her to get ready for bed and that she would bring the tea up to her. As Vera sat down wearily, Susie went over to her and stroked her hand.

'Vera, please try not to worry now, try to think good thoughts and a peaceful sleep will make you better, I think.'

Downstairs, Mrs. Wilson spoke to Miss Swift on the phone. They both agreed that Vera should have an appointment with Doctor Perrins as soon as possible. He came weekly to Rosebank and knew all the residents. He had once interviewed Vera when she came first, after her referral by her GP. He was surprised at the referral, as he did not agree that Vera was in the early stages of dementia at all.

Eva decided not to worry Judy just now. After the doctor's visit and depending on what he thought, would be time enough. The woman had enough on her plate, Eva thought.

The night staff was advised to check on Vera at some stage during the night to make sure she was alright.

Vera slept fitfully and had horrible dreams. It seemed she was visiting Judy in hospital, over and over and Vera could not get close enough to speak with her. She was bathed in sweat when she woke up at seven o'clock. Getting out of bed with difficulty she stumbled into the bathroom and sat in her shower and let the water cascade over her, hoping it would wash away all the troubled thoughts that were in her mind.

She pulled herself together and got dressed for breakfast. In the dining room, Ivy came over and sat by her. The little woman was worried by the change she saw in her friend. Something bad had happened her, she knew. They ate in silence. Ivy told Vera that she was always there to listen when she wanted to talk. Vera nodded and smiled at Ivy.

'You will hear my story, just as soon as I feel able Ivy. I have had a shock, that's all.'

When she went for her medication, Maura looked closely at her. She told her that there was an appointment with Doctor Perrins that afternoon at three o'clock. When Vera protested that Monday was the singalong day, Maura shook her head.

'Vera, you have had a shock, so Mrs. Wilson has told me. It would be better to get a check-up as soon as possible. We want you well, and able to continue with the music, all the residents are feeling the benefit you know. We have all noticed a marked improvement in everybody since these singalong afternoons. She smiled at the haggard-looking woman in front of her. There was certainly a facial change in Vera. Maura wondered if she could have suffered a minor stroke.

Vera wandered back to the lounge and sat looking out the window. She felt someone sit down next to her and looked up to find Jack Stroke there.

'You alright, Vera? We were all a bit worried about you.'

Vera sighed. 'Yes, it was such a lovely concert and I enjoyed it so much. Then I got some bad news, Jack from a woman I knew years ago. It's hard to take in and I really felt awful after hearing it.'

Jack made no comment, he just patted her hand as it lay on her lap.

'It concerns my daughter, Jack. She has got involved with a bad one it appears, and I am very worried about it all.'

'How old is Judy, Vera?' asked Jack gently.

'Well, she is forty-four.'

'And do you not think that she is old enough to sort out her problems? She is a mature woman Vera, and a mother. She will cope, don't you worry. She will find out just what sort of man he is and get rid of him.'

Vera sighed. 'I hope so, Jack. It's the boys that I am more worried about.'

Jack nodded. 'I don't think we ever consider our children grown up, even when they have children. You cannot help her by worrying about things. You must try to step back. She has to be allowed to make her decisions and choices, rightly or wrongly.'

Vera stood up. 'You are of course correct, Jack. I will try and do as you advise. I am off now for a walk around the garden. They want me to see Doctor Perrins this afternoon, so I won't be there for our usual singsong.'

'No harm Vera, I think everyone is still bushed after both the Friday night shenanigans and yesterday's concert. Don't worry about that. We will all be in better form on Thursday.

Vera went in to see the doctor at three. She did not feel so bad now as before. Talking about it helped, she thought.

The doctor saw a deterioration in the woman before him. He suspected that something had happened in her brain, possibly brought on by the bad news that Mrs. Wilson said she had received.

He carried out numerous tests which she passed without difficulty. He asked her about the shock she had got.

Vera tried to make light of it. Family problems, she told him. She was a bit worried about her daughter's new relationship, having heard bad things about the man.

He said the same things, more-or-less, that Jack had told her. Judy was an adult and would sort herself out in time. He told her that he would like to see her again in a couple of weeks and not to hesitate to speak with the nurse if she should feel ill or out of sorts again.

After asking her about how she slept and her appetite, he recommended a mild sedative for night and morning.

Vera was quite sure that she did not need a sedative but refrained from making an issue of it.

Mrs. Wilson had also asked her to drop into her office when her session with Perrins was over, so

Vera went straight in and decided to get that over with.

Mrs. Wilson was a sensitive person and was worried about Vera's appearance too. She sat the woman down and quietly enquired about her shock.

Vera had no trouble relaying the story that Molly told her. She also told Mrs. Wilson, that she had intended to ask her weeks ago, whether she should return home to help Judy. But now, with a strange man in the house, she knew it could not happen.

Eva Wilson agreed with her, also reiterating the advice Jack had given her. She told Vera to ring her daughter as often as she wished and encourage her to visit.

'Everyone has problems here, Vera. They don't disappear just because you are in a retirement home, believe me.'

By suppertime, Vera was feeling a lot better and was able to play bridge that evening, partnering Mr. Burrow. Duncan Power played with Sylvie and Ivy played draughts with Bob Grunt. Everyone was occupied with either cards, other games, or watching television.

Maggie spoke again about Friday night and how she thought that it was the best night yet. People nodded in agreement.

Sylvie, overhearing and watching Vera shuffle the cards, called over, 'I have never enjoyed a night like it, for the first time since coming here, I felt as free as a bird and ridiculously young.'

Chapter 22

The singsongs resumed that Thursday, and half the time was spent revising and practicing Christmas carols. Ivy was going to do a solo and then a duet with Jack Stroke. Maggie had the song sheets all printed out and in a folder for everyone. Vera asked if anyone played an instrument and there was a flurry of excitement. Maisie had once played the violin but was very out of practice, she said. Maggie asked if she could get it from her family and start practicing. Sylvie had a flute and offered to bring it to practice it too. It had lain in its box for many years, but she had been loathe to throw it out, and had packed it when coming to the house. Maggie was pleased with her organising skills. Vera had still not recovered completely and was subdued these days. She had spoken to Mrs. Wilson about her and asked if she needed any particular help. The woman had replied that at first a mini stroke was suspected but as the days passed, this was dismissed. She would recover in her own time, Eva said.

Vera continued her walks each day around the grounds even though the autumn was now well in progress and the trees were becoming barer. Still, the air was bracing, and she knew that she must make the effort to function normally.

The next day a letter arrived from Charlie and Vera quickly took it to read outside in the wan sunshine that morning. He was settled in school. He was still worried about his brothers. He was looking forward to going home for Halloween. He finished by telling her that he would be in touch soon again and might even be able to come and visit her over the half term holiday.

She hugged the letter to herself. She knew that he was a sensible and grounded boy and hoped that the twins would turn out as well grounded.

As she sat and pondered her situation, Jack Stroke and Bob came along, Susie pushing Bob. They came alongside Vera and asked her to go for a stroll with them.

Jack was keeping an eye on Vera too and thought he saw an improvement. Jack noted that it was just two months since Ken had died. He wondered where the time went. Bob grunted that the fellow should have died years ago, and Jack laughed. Vera wondered what it was that Bob had against Ken. She was feeling curious again and decided that meant she was better, and she determined to find out from Jack.

The chance came later that night. It was a quiet night, and nobody was playing cards. There was a new series on the television that the oldies wanted to see. Jack was sitting reading the paper in his usual corner and Vera came and sat next to him.

'I am curious as hell, Jack. What had Bob got against the Lech?'

Jack took off his reading glasses and turned to her.

'Do you remember me telling you about his wife running away with the bass guitarist?'

Vera nodded.

'Well that was Ken the Lech. He always had an eye for the ladies, did Ken. However, he had his nose put out of joint when someone else took her fancy. He lost her to a bank manager.' He winked at Vera and smiled.

'Bob never got over the hurt though, which is understandable. He is a decent bloke and was always joking and laughing, not that you would suspect that, looking at him today.'

'Poor Bob, how harshly we judge people, not knowing about their troubles.'

'Yep, Bob is a first-class bloke and very sincere. He doesn't talk much anymore, but with the singsongs and dance nights, he has come out of himself a lot.'

'You seem to know a lot about everyone here, Jack. Are you from the town or the outlying area?'

'I'm from the town Vera, and most of us here are, so of course, if we did not know each other personally, we certainly know of them. Nothing goes unnoticed in a small town, you know.'

'Well I am from Killyvant, so it's far enough away. Judy picked here because it was modern, and she said much better than some of the retirement homes that she researched. So, I have never met or known any of the residents.'

'You might be as well off, Vera. Sometimes you can know too much, and it can be awkward.'

Vera did not ask him what he meant. There was a mass exodus from the television room and lots of grumbling.

'Honestly, the things they put on the screen now, its' disgraceful.' Maisie had a long face on her. 'Why was it necessary to do nude scenes at all, does anyone know?'

There was clicking of tongues and head wagging. Some of the men winked at each other and were not too loud in their protestations. Vera smiled to herself. Some of the old dears would probably be shocked to see anything bared above the knee.

'It's supposed to be a reflection of modern life today, and how things have changed,' someone remarked.

'Sure, there was always sex before marriage, adultery and incest, nothing new there,' was another comment.

'And now there is the new one, "Gay", where will it all end?'

Someone laughed heartily. 'Sure, gay is just another word for queer, or homosexual. That was always in existence, from the beginning of time, people just didn't talk about it and pretended it didn't exist. They still don't talk about it, to do so would be considered bad taste.'

'Well I don't think that they should use the word 'gay', after all, that means happy and lighthearted, doesn't it? Does it mean that those type of people are always happy and laughing?'

Mr. Burrow coughed loudly and said it was time for his bed and left the lounge.

Sylvie glared at the person who made the last remark. 'Some people have no sensitivity,' she declared, 'and are ignorant into the bargain.'

Vera was surprised at this exchange. Frankly, she was not interested in people's private or sex lives. Her motto had always been, 'Live and let live'. There was hardly ever this sort of chat and ideas spoken about so clearly and Vera thought that the lively exchange was not a bad thing. It meant that they were still able to think!

The art lesson that week was well attended, although Duncan was not there. He was finding it difficult to adjust to his hearing aids and was constantly fiddling with them. It made him more crotchety than ever. Susie and Annie were great with him and so patient. Susie was beside Ivy at the lesson and they were very intent on what they were doing, listening to Paul's instructions. He had brought a middle-aged woman to sit as a model for them and they were requested to try and get her likeness with pencils or charcoal. Vera found it quite difficult and

146

looking at other results around her, felt an irresistible urge to laugh. She smothered it into a giggle and Maggie came over to see how she was getting on.

'Vera, you've made the poor woman look half starved, what's happened her chest, then?'

Paul laughed at them and said that first efforts were always a hoot. The model smiled and told them that she would not take offence. Only Ivy and Susie's sketches bore any resemblance to the model and again, Paul took an interest in them and mentioned various tips that they could try.

The evenings followed the same routine and the days rolled along. Sometimes it was difficult to remember which day it was, except for the weekends.

Maggie and the two Jacks huddled together a lot and Vera knew that they were discussing the next dance night.

There was to be another dance night this Friday and Vera hoped that she would be up to it. It was two weeks since the last one and energy levels were high again. Jack asked around for any spare sleeping tablets and was happy with what he collected.

Vera had a letter from Judy. She was going to visit this coming Sunday. Vera was delighted but also a bit apprehensive about the situation at home. Maybe it was all resolved. She hoped so.

Maggie had the Christmas carols and programmes printed at the office and Mrs. Wilson was notified of the agenda. She would be inviting some important people she told Maggie, like the Mayor and his wife, and the local politicians. It was always beneficial for the outside world to see how these retirement homes operated. Invitations were issued to all relatives too.

Chapter 23

The weather had turned suddenly chilly with lots of rain and wind. The house was kept well heated however and the residents were told to wrap up warmly going out for their walks.

The usual routine was followed on Friday. Everyone had a siesta, and then left the lounge shortly after nine. Tonight, it was Bob Grunt and Mr. Burrow who were to make the two on duty do a lot of running around. They had planned what they would do and hoped the two men would be tired out after it all.

Maggie insisted that she could not pull the same stunt again and that it would be highly suspicious if she did.

Mr. Burrow began by going out the front door into the garden. It was dark by now but a moonlit night and was just before the doors automatically locked.

After ten minutes, Bob called Mano and told him that he was worried as Mr. Burrow was not in his room and someone had seen him go out the front door some time ago.

That caused a bit of panic and Mano put on his coat and went out to look for him. Sid said he would put the water out in the bedrooms and to hurry back. Then Jack Other discovered a leak in his bathroom and Sid had to go and investigate that. True, there was a lot of water on the floor, but he could not find out where it could have come from. He checked the taps in the basin and looked in the shower. The toilet was flushing alright, but he had to wait until it refilled to check again. He told Jack he would write a memo about it and leave in on the secretary's desk in the office. Then Maggie was misfortunate enough to knock her carafe of water off her locker. Poor Sid was running here there and all around the place. When Mano had still not come back after more than forty minutes, he had to put on his coat and go out and look for him. He found Mr. Burrow on the bench beneath the oak tree with Mano. He was pointing to the brightly shining stars and patiently showing Mano the different constellations. The man was genuinely interested in what Mr. Burrow was saying and was too polite to insist on the man returning to the house.

It was only when Sid appeared around a corner and shouted, 'What the bloody hell….' that Mano suddenly realised that they should not be out here at all.

Sid was furious with Mano. Mr. Burrow, suspecting that he may have got the man into trouble tried to pour oil on the troubled water.

'So sorry Sid, I should have asked you first. It was such a wonderful bright night after all that rain, and I am very fascinated by the night skies. It is not often that you see such a clear sky and just look at the moon, isn't it wonderful?'

He looked as if he meant to stay sitting on the bench, until Sid roughly grabbed his arm and pulled him to his feet. Mr. Burrow was alarmed at this handling and started to remonstrate.

'Listen Burrow, if you want to sit under the moon with Mano, just don't do it when we are so busy, right?'

He glared at Mano and the three started back to the house, Mr. Burrow walked slowly, and Mano kept pace with him whereas Sid strode off angrily.

Eventually the house quietened, and the two men went to dinner. Jack Stroke did his technical work again in the office and sauntered back to bed with a mug of tea.

The Friday night followed the usual routine. All gathered quietly and doors were closed, and curtains and blinds drawn. Vera started gently as she always did, some old-time waltzes and gentle foxtrots. Bob softly accompanied her on his two drums. It sounded good. After a while they all wanted some faster stuff, not just Sylvie. Several people tried to do the tango as they remembered Ivy and Sylvie doing it. Maggie pushed Maisie in her wheelchair, turning fast and running backwards and forwards and making Maisie laugh and clap her hands. The Zimmer frames helped some to move a bit faster too. At last there were requests for some music from Mamma Mia. Mr. Burrow and Ivy strutted around the room smartly to "Super Trouper", Sylvie and Jack Other went mad to

"Money, Money, Money", and eventually it was Jack Stroke who hushed them and said that they were worse that teenagers and time was up.

They quietly gathered themselves together and left silently. Jack and Mr. Burrow and Vera were the last to leave. They opened the curtains and blinds, tidied the chairs as best they could and left.

When Vera had disappeared to her wing, the two men hovered and listened outside the staff room door. There was no sound. Jack tried the office: there was nobody there. He slipped in to do his magic. Mr. Burrow kept watch. Suddenly the staff room door opened, and Sid the Snake emerged rubbing his eyes. Mr. Burrow froze like a rabbit caught in the headlights of a car. He coughed loudly.

'Well, well, if it isn't Mr. Burrow. And what, may I ask are you doing here at this time of night? Looking for Mano, are you? Well he is not interested in you, old man. He has a girlfriend you know. He's not your type.' He laughed scornfully and looked Mr. Burrow up and down.

'N-n not at all, I only came to get c-cup of tea. I am finding it hard to sleep tonight.' Poor Mr. Burrow was quite put out and so nervous that he did not know what to say.

Sid went quite close to the man. 'I have been inquiring about you for some time. I know all about you, Burrow. I have heard the story about when you were a teacher. There was a complaint about you, isn't that right? A child complained, I believe.'

'That is not true! That was over forty years ago and there was no child involved. The young man was a teacher too and in his twenties. It was a mistake I made, I misread the signals and I have paid for it.'

'Well now, Burrow or Rabbit as you are known, I don't know how Mrs. Wilson or any of the residents would feel about that. I might have to disclose it, you know. Of course, if you could see your way to drop a fifty euro note my way, now and again, it could be that I might forget I ever heard the story.'

Sid smirked at the man and went straight to the kitchen, which was off the dining room.

When he was gone, Mr. Burrow tapped on the office door. Jack opened the office door and listened. There was no sound. He nodded at Mr. Burrow to go which he did. He waited a while, knowing that Sid would be returning. He heard the man pass the office door and return to the staff room.

'Mano, come on, wakey wakey, time to play cards again. You have won too much tonight. I have to win it back, man.'

Only then did Jack leave the office and return to his wing.

Chapter 24

On Sunday afternoon Vera had her visitor. It was a dry but cold day. They took a walk around the grounds. Judy came alone but promised a proper family visit in a couple of weeks.

She confided in her mother that Tommy was rather wonderful and caring. He was also a great cook and she was constantly surprised on coming home after a day's work, to find a lovely supper waiting for her.

Vera asked about the boys and how they were doing. Judy thought that they were adjusting well. Anyway, they had so many extracurricular activities that they and Tommy were not together too much. She was a bit worried about Charlie coming at half term and hoped he would be civil.

'Please Mum, be happy for me. It's wonderful to have someone in my life again that cares for me.'

Vera took her arm. 'My dearest girl, I want you to be happy. It's what every mother wants for her child. It is just that the warning I got was so awful, that I panicked and feared the worst: that he would be manipulative and controlling. The abuse report really bothered me.'

'Tommy has had a hard time. He told me all about his ex-wife. She is no saint Mum, believe me. He really wants us to be a family a normal family and I believe him and trust him.'

Well, after that Vera felt mighty relieved. Things were not as bad as she suspected. There are two sides to every story, she supposed and who was she to judge? If Judy felt safe with him, then it surely was alright.

She secreted the bottle of whiskey that Judy brought into her large holdall. They went inside and enjoyed their afternoon tea. Ivy came over and Vera introduced her to Judy.

'Your mother has brought us all alive here, Judy. Has she told you?'

Judy shook her head and looked inquiringly at her mother.

Vera just laughed and told her daughter about the singsong afternoons. She frowned at Ivy over her daughter's head as Ivy looked as though she might divulge more. Ivy understood and excused herself and went over to sit with Jack Stroke and Jack Other.

'You are sure you are alright here, Mum? It was supposed to be temporary and this romance was not planned, I assure you. It just kind of happened.'

'That's life, Judy. Things just happen. I like it here but as you say, it was supposed to be temporary and I shall have to adjust my thinking again and adapt.'

Judy sighed. 'I know you would not be comfortable back home now with Tommy present, but something could be done, maybe a Granny flat or extension. What do you think?'

'I will think about it, Judy. I am fine here for the moment. It's rather like a hotel; the food is wonderful, and the people are generally all mentally well. There are a couple of sick ninety-year-olds, over in the big house. We play bridge in the evenings, have singsongs and really, I can't ask for more at my age, can I? I'm afraid I am not up to gardening anymore and I really couldn't see myself cooking for a family and housekeeping. Those days are over Judy. I have slowed down quite a bit but feel mentally alright, like most of the inmates here.'

She said goodbye to Judy and did not feel as stressed as she thought she would. Plus, she now had her bottle of whiskey and that was something to look forward to at night.

After hiding the bottle in the toilet cistern, she went down to supper in a strong frame of mind.

They were all present and chattering. After supper, Sylvie asked Vera if she felt like bridge, or was she too tired?

'Not tired at all Sylvie, let us go and play.'

The lounge was full, and nobody seemed to want to watch television. The ladies especially, were all full of the Friday night's clandestine activity. Maggie announced that she no longer suffered any hip or joint pains, and she knew that the dancing was the reason.

'Wouldn't it be great if they allowed us to dance during the week, the way we do on Friday night?'

Jack Stroke shook his head. 'No way, girl. I told you before! It's because of the insurance on the place. If one of us broke wind, never mind a hip, the insurance premiums would triple and we, none of us, would be able to afford to stay here. Mark my words.'

That quietened them. They all knew that they were in a special place and appreciated how they were so well treated and fed.

Sylvie requested the game to start and immediately asked where Mr. Burrow was? Everyone looked around. He was not in the lounge. Then Jack Other remarked that he had not seen him at supper. They all looked at each other. Maggie offered to go and see if he was in his room. Being able to move faster than most of the others, she took off.

Duncan told Sylvie that he would play with her. Then he asked why his damn hearing aids squealed so much? He spent all his time now, fiddling with them, eventually taking them out and putting them in his pocket.

'Maybe you have them turned up too high, Dennis,' Sylvie suggested, 'try turning them down a little.'
The two of them looked at the offending hearing aids and Sylvie showed him how to turn them down.

Vera looked around for Ivy, but she was missing too.

Oh dear, it looked like a non-bridge night, she thought.

After some time, Maggie returned to the lounge. She looked rather pale and agitated. She sat down beside the two Jacks. Jack Stroke asked her if she had located Rabbit? She nodded, biting her lip.

'Well, is he not coming down then? It's not like him to miss a game of bridge with the lovely Sylvie.'

'Oh Jack! I don't know what to think. Poor Mr. Burrow is so upset, and I don't know what is wrong with him. I found him crying, can you believe that Jack. A grown man crying like a little boy. I feel quite sick.'

Jack looked at Maggie in alarm. 'Is he all by himself up there in his room? Did you leave him like that?'

'Of course not! Ivy is with him and seems to be able to comfort him. I just left in shock.'

She wrung her hands and looked ready to cry herself. 'What can we do Jack?'

Jack Stroke did not answer her. He looked straight ahead, and his face looked quite grim, unlike his usual friendly smiley face. Maggie wished she had not gone up to Mr. Burrow's room and witnessed what she had seen.

Vera looked over at Maggie and raised her eyebrows. Sylvie and Dennis were again checking the hearing aids and were totally engrossed.

Maggie shook her head and got to her feet.

'Good night all,' she muttered before leaving the room.

After she had left, Vera sat at the table with Duncan and Sylvie. 'Well it seems that there is a shortage of bridge players tonight, which is a pity. But perhaps tomorrow night if all are well?'

She felt a movement behind her and started in surprise as Ivy sat down beside her.

'Well Ivy, are we going to play after all?'

Ivy nodded and apologised for keeping them waiting. 'Mr. Burrow is indisposed and cannot play tonight, Sylvie.'

'Oh, that's alright, as Duncan is going to play. Shall we start?'

The problem with the hearing aids having been sorted, the four settled down and tonight, Ivy was in her element. Vera had never seen her play so well and so confidently. She did not make one mistake and was so aggressive in her play that Vera wondered if she herself was losing it. How could she have been so mistaken in her judgement of Ivy?

Chapter 25

Winter was well on the way now. The trees were all bare and the gardens devoid of colour. Only the evergreen trees and shrubs stood out, giving an air of solemnity and mystery to the landscape. Life in the house seemed a little more subdued too. There were more activities it was true; two afternoons a week some volunteers came from the town and entertained the residents. There was indoor bowling in the recreation room which the men enjoyed and an hour of storytelling from one of the teachers from town, from well-known books of short stories, which most of the women loved. Vera's singsongs continued and the art classes too.

Halloween was approaching and the children from the nearby school were preparing to come trick and treating in their neighbourhood. They also included Rosebank House at the end of their evening where they were assured of lots of cakes and soft drinks and were then sent home with bags of sweets. The custom had begun five years ago, and everyone enjoyed the evening. Before the children came around at eight o'clock, there were games held in the recreation room and people were encouraged to dress up a bit. Mrs. Wilson entered into the spirit of things and always dressed up as a witch. In the week beforehand, bags of clothing were sorted out and everyone took what they wanted to dress up in.

Those who were not able to, were helped by staff members. Susie and Annie loved this time of the year, the air of excitement and sense of joy, which they knew would be followed by a quiet period before the Christmas celebrations. It was also the time when some people fell ill with the usual winter colds and flu, a time when there was more activity between the old house and the newer Rosebank. Seriously sick residents would be quarantined in the big house, to safeguard others; this scared some of the oldies, their worry being whether they would get back to their own room again.

This morning after breakfast Miss Swift announced that the flu injection would be administered by the doctor, when the usual medicines were given out.

After getting their jabs, Vera and Jack Stroke took a walk around the gardens. They were fresh air enthusiasts and believed that their immunity depended on it.

'The central heating was way too high last night,' complained Jack. 'The lounge was much too hot, do you think, Vera?'

'I do, Jack. It was stifling in there and I was nodding off before nine. Do you think we could ask them to regulate it better?'

'No harm in asking, is there? I'll mention it to Sweety when we go back.'

On their return they met Mr. Burrow, all muffled up with scarf and hat and gloves.

He nodded at them in passing. Jack would have stopped but knew that Mr. Burrow did not intend to slow his pace.

'Is he alright, do you think. He's not the same as he was, somehow, or is it my imagination Jack?'

'No, you're right, something is bugging the fellow.'

'Oh well, I suppose we are all changing slowly. I've noticed a few of the oldies are getting more forgetful, but then again, so am I,' laughed Vera.

'Well all we can do is mind ourselves, Vera, winter is a bad time for us all. Now, here we are, and I intend to go straight to Sweety Swift and tell her that stuffy lounges are not conducive to healthy residents, and Vera, turn down the heat in your bedroom too, a hot bedroom is deadly.'

'Don't worry Jack, I never have the heat on at night. I might turn the radiator on for a couple of hours in the afternoon, but it's off when I retire for the night.'

That afternoon was art class and for once Vera was not too interested. She felt like lying in bed and reading and decided that that is what she would do.

Later in the evening they were all in the lounge as usual except for a couple of oldies who were now more inclined to go to bed after supper. Whether it was the dark evenings that affected them more or just age, the staff always noticed a change in the winter months.

Tonight, there was a bridge game going on and the Jacks were playing chess. The television had been giving some trouble lately and when the news time came, there were some vocal mutterings. Jack Stroke rang the bell to summon help and after a few minutes Sid came in. He fiddled with the television and managed to get the thing sorted. On his way out, he paused by the bridge table and stood opposite Mr. Burrow. Eventually the man looked up and caught his eye. His face paled visibly. Play was held up and the other three also looked at Mr. Burrow to see what was holding him up.

'When you are finished your game, *Mister* Burrow, I'd like a word in your ear. I'll be in the office.'

Vera did not like the tone of Sid's voice and muttered 'rude man', under her breath.

'Yes absolutely, rude and ignorant, I do not like that man,' Sylvie said, playing her final trump, and winning a difficult hand, with great skill.

'Oh well done, partner! That was magnificent play.' Duncan was elated and quite relieved that he was not the one having to play the hand.

Vera thanked Mr. Burrow for playing with her. He did not seem to hear her but rose quickly and left the room.

Sylvie feeling very invigorated by her win, looked at the remaining two and asked, 'what on earth does that man Sid, want with Mr. Burrow, I wonder?'

Vera shook her head. Duncan appeared not to have heard the question. Jack Stroke having seen the news was just entering as Sylvie's voice boomed out.

'What was that about Sid and Rabbit?' He looked from Sylvie to Vera.

Sylvie recounted the rude interruption and Sid's request, which has seemed more like a demand.

Now other people were listening to the exchange and looking puzzled. Ivy asked where Mr. Burrow was now. 'Probably gone to see what that man wants, I imagine.'

Now people were yawning and standing up and straightening their stiff limbs. The heating had been lowered tonight and they were all pleased, except Bob Grunt who loved heat and moaned most of the evening.

On their way to their rooms they looked towards the office but did not see Mr. Burrow. Some went to make tea or cocoa and to sit and chat quietly in the dining room before turning in, Sylvie, Ivy and Vera among them.

Ivy looked around nervously. 'I do hope poor Mr. Burrow is alright. Sid gets him all agitated, I feel.'

Sylvie sighed. 'He's a grown man for heaven's sake, Ivy and well able to take care of himself I'm sure.'

Vera told the two women that she was expecting Judy and the three boys to visit before Halloween and how much she was looking forward to seeing them.

Ivy told the two ladies that she was going to bring Mr. Burrow up a cup of tea to his room and make sure he was alright.

Chapter 26

Thursday came with a blue sky and watery sunshine. Vera ate her breakfast quickly and went a brisk walk before getting her medicine. She was excited at the prospect of visitors but also nervous. She hoped that things were working out for Judy and the boys.

After the exercise class, there was a scramble for Halloween costumes and hats. Sylvie complained that there was never anything big enough to fit her well and Ivy moaned that she could find nothing small enough. Vera grabbed a scarlet floor length cloak and black leggings.

'That's nice,' Sylvie said. 'What or who are you going to be?'

'I am soon to be Mrs. Dracula. I may have to borrow your red lipstick to daub a bit of 'blood' on my chin, Sylvie.'

'Oh, you are so imaginative. What can I dress up as?' Poor Ivy rooted through the jumble laid out on a table.

'Look Ivy, here's the very thing for you. This emerald two piece would look great on you, you can be a leprechaun.'

They surveyed the waistcoat and trousers and agreed. It must have belonged to a child, Vera thought.

Ivy was as excited as if she won the lotto. 'I have a yellow blouse that I could wear under the waistcoat.'

Sylvie sniffed and tossed her head. 'You will look like a fairy that's jumped off the Christmas tree. But what about me, what will I do?'

Vera and Ivy rummaged around. It was Ivy who found what she thought was wonderful: a full-length bridal veil. There was no dress, however. Vera put the veil on Sylvie's head and Ivy and herself smiled and told Sylvie that she must wear it.

'With what, may I ask? There is nothing here in my size. What will I wear with it, my nightdress?'

Even as she said it, she knew that she had the answer. 'Why of course, my new dressing gown that I swore I would never wear, seeing as my daughter-in-law sent it for my birthday.'

Nobody had seen it and of course the three at once had to go to Sylvie's room to see the object. It was in a rich purple silky material in a kimono style. Ivy and Vera were open-mouthed with admiration.

'Sylvie, that is so beautiful. It is absolutely stunning.' Ivy had never seen anything so rich or lovely.

Vera agreed. 'It's very exotic Sylvie, you must go as the bride of either Dracula or Frankenstein. Oh, you can't go as the bride of Dracula as I'm going as Mrs. Dracula.' The three roared with laughter.

The three were happy with their choices and Ivy went to her room to try on her costume.

At three o'clock, Vera's visitors arrived, and all moved to the dining room for afternoon tea. The boys looked well and had grown. Charlie was growing so tall; Vera could hardly believe it. The talk was mainly about school and sports events and the coming holiday weekend. Vera told them about their party weekend coming up and the costumes they would dress up in. The twins thought it was hilarious that old people would do that.

She told them about the school children who would come trick treating and how they would have to provide some entertainment for the old people before they got their treats.

Vera wondered when Tommy's name would come up. She then asked Judy what she would do for Halloween if the three boys were all off to parties.

'I'll have a quiet night in Mum and hope the doorbell won't ring all night.'

Vera saw a scowl on Charlie's face and the glance that passed between the three boys. She made no comment.

As they walked around the grounds, just before Judy departed, Vera asked softly about Tommy.

'Is the romance still going on?'

Judy shot a look at the boys and then nodded her head. She then told the boys to go ahead to the car and take out the bag in the boot for Granny. When they had departed, she told her mother that Tommy was as attentive as ever and she hoped that the boys would be won over eventually.

'You know boys, Mum, so protective of their mother and a bit resentful of another man in her life. All will be well in time, I'm sure.'

Vera secreted the paper bag into her holdall and hugged them all in turn.

'Do drop me a line from time to time,' she urged them. 'Nobody writes letters anymore and I cannot manage these mobile things.'

They agreed to do that and continued waving from the car windows as they drove away.

Vera walked up to her room feeling sad for the boys. She knew by their manner that there was a tension there that had not been present before. She put her bottle of whiskey in its usual hiding place.

That night in the lounge, Mad Maggie had a great idea that she relayed to the others in great excitement.

'Listen all of you. This Friday is Halloween as you all know, and the visiting children will all be gone home by nine-thirty or so. What do you all think about having our own Halloween party afterwards, while we are still in fancy dress? She beamed around at them all expectantly.

There was no doubting by the response, that they all agreed it was a great idea. Jack Stroke was a bit dubious. There would be a lot of coming and going after the children's visit as extra volunteers and staff would be employed for the event.

Sylvie thought that the house would settle down even quicker after all that. The staff and volunteers would be anxious to get home and finish off their private celebrations in their own homes.

Ivy nodded her head as did most of the others.

After a few more arguments in favour of their own party night, it was finally decided: Friday night would again see the residents of Rosebank jiving and having a great time.

Mr. Burrow had been unusually quiet during the conversation. Ivy, sitting beside him, asked what he thought of it. He was totally noncommittal which was unusual, neither showing any great interest nor being against the idea either.

Ivy was disappointed and looked over at Jack Stroke, who frowned slightly and shook his head.

They all left for bed shortly afterwards. Jack walked beside Ivy. 'Don't bother the man, I'll get around him, I know him well and he loves our dances. Don't worry, he'll be there.'

Everyone went to bed feeling excited. The local hairdresser was coming tomorrow as she usually did on Friday. Not every lady had her hair done weekly, but this weekend, most of them would splash out and not only the ladies. Sylvie was a weekly recipient and had her nails done fortnightly. Ivy rarely did but was getting her hair done tomorrow as was Vera and most of the others.

Mrs. Wilson had her breakfast next morning with the residents. She was excited too and mentioned that the Mayor was going to make an appearance while the children were present. She was always eager to show off her 'family' as she called them and let the outside world know that they existed and happily.

The only downside was that one of the old ladies who was in a wheelchair had to be moved to the big house early in the morning with flu symptoms. Being the season it was, more would possibly succumb to the winter scourge. She urged them all to ask for vitamin pills if they felt they needed them. In fact, she was going to see Nurse Maura herself and mention it to her.

The day went by quickly and soon it was time to dress up. Susie and Annie volunteered for extra duty and Susie's sister, a nurse, also came to help. Not many had their afternoon siesta that Friday.

They were all in the recreation room having a singsong and playing games until the time the children would come. Their games were adapted to their needs. One favourite game was hitting apples into an open box lying on its side, using walking sticks. Jack Stroke kept winning of course.

'I always knew my golf would come in handy,' he chortled. Those on Zimmer frames used them to try their luck. There was much laughter. Tables were laid with soft drinks and plates of sweets and biscuits.

After a while, they all sat down. Vera played some old time favourites and they began to sing.

Eva Wilson got up and sang a song to start off the soloists, knowing that if she broke the ice everyone would get over their shyness at her presence. She had a lovely warm voice and got a ringing applause.

Maggie took the plunge. Her voice was so deep that Vera was surprised every time she heard it. The two Jacks of course loved performing: both basses and their voices complimented each other, and they always found a funny song that had everyone laughing their heads off. Tonight, they sang that song from Mary Poppins: "Supercalifragilistic".
Tears were running down most faces when it finally finished. Jack Other did a bit of dancing while Jack Stroke beat time with his stick.

Someone asked Susie to sing and she shook her head shyly, but Annie volunteered to sing with her so, they did. A quick word with Vera and a couple of notes tried, then they softly sang "Somewhere over the Rainbow" and sat down happy and flushed.

Then Maggie demanded that Ivy sing "My Lagan love", which she did willingly.

There was perfect quiet when she sang the haunting melody, it was always a mystery how someone so slight could have such an amazing voice.

As she finished, there was commotion and people started murmuring that the Mayor was coming now.

Then the children also arrived, and the residents sat down and were entertained. There was ballet, tap dancing, Irish dancing all types of songs and singers and the hour went by quickly.

Vera was glad to hand over the piano to others. There was also a small school band which played a wonderful selection of traditional tunes.

At last the children all exited after a short speech of thanks by the Mayor and then a responding one from Eva Wilson.

It was now ten o'clock and later than had been anticipated. Jack Stroke and Jack Other conferred with Maggie and agreed it should still go on.

They had had enough tea and snacks all evening and went straight to their rooms. Sid was standing watching them all go and told them he had delivered water to their rooms. Mr. Burrow hurried past him with his head down. Ivy followed and Sid looked at her strangely she thought. He looked as if he had swallowed something nasty, she thought.

Silence followed. At midnight, the bedroom doors opened slowly, and the dressed-up residents softly made their way down to the recreation room again, which had been tidied up since the earlier party. Maggie and a couple of others went around bringing chairs into a line on one side of the piano.

Jack Stroke told Vera to remind him to turn on the CCTV on their return.

Chapter 27

Sylvie requested a tango immediately, as she did not know how long her energy would last. Jack Stroke intervened then and insisted she remove her veil, which could cause a nasty accident, he said. She obeyed him, smiling at him with her big childlike eyes.

The others loved watching this spectacle and Vera wished the piano faced the other way so that she could see it too. She only got a glimpse on one side. Ivy looked so cute in her leprechaun outfit. Again, they looked an incongruous couple, the purple kimono clad Sylvie and the green and yellow clad Ivy, tangoing for all they were worth and oblivious of the amusement of the others.

Then they were all up and doing their own thing. It was not as energetic as before, Vera felt. Possibly they were tired by the other party and no siesta. Still, there were calls for more rock and roll and finally the old-time waltzes were played, and conversations became quieter.

At last Jack Stroke called an end to the evening and told everyone to return quietly and sleep well.

They all walked slowly to bed. In truth, they were all exhausted. It has been a long day and a lot of excitement too. Jack Other led the line of elderly people and as he neared the reception area, held up his hand. They all stopped still and wondered what he was waiting for. Then they heard the front door open and got a glimpse of Mano dressed in his outdoor coat, hurrying into the night with his head down.

Jack Other came back and whispered that Mano must be going to the big house to help out. They waited a further few minutes and when nothing more was heard, proceeded to their bedrooms.

Jack Stroke nipped into the office and quickly did his work on the CCTV. Vera waited outside to make sure he was not disturbed.

On reaching her room, Vera wearily took off her shoes and disrobed. Everyone had looked the part for the celebrations and their costumes had been admired by the children who were amazed at adults dressing up too.

She was bone weary though. As she dressed for bed, she remembered her whiskey and got her glass. On opening the toilet cistern, she found it lacking a bottle of whiskey. She could not believe it. She looked again and then checked every drawer and cupboard in her room, knowing it in her heart it had been stolen again. She felt frustrated and angry. It was so unfair.

She got into bed and put out the light. She lay awake, wondering what she could do about the theft. Someone had seen that she had visitors yesterday and took the opportunity. She had opened the bottle last night and had a drink, she had wanted to make this bottle last until Judy could come again, and heaven knew when that would be. Eventually she slept. It was a disturbed sleep though, she thought she could hear strange sounds. Must be Mano coming back from the big house was her last thought before falling into a deeper sleep.

The residents of Rosebank woke early that Saturday morning. Doors were being banged and hurried footsteps. Looking out of her window, Vera could see nothing. Maggie on the other wing saw an ambulance parked and a police car. She was still half asleep, but curiosity got the better of her and she dressed and wandered down to the dining room. She was met by a distraught Eva Wilson who asked her if she would mind returning to her room for a while as something terrible had happened.

As she turned to go, she met Jack Other coming along and passed on the message. They looked at each other in alarm.

'God, I hope Sylvie has not had a stroke, after all that dancing,' he muttered.

Maggie paled. 'Oh no! I hope not. She did a lot of dancing I thought. I wondered how she had the energy after the earlier evening.'

'What should we do?' wondered Jack Other.

'As we're told. Back to our rooms and see if anyone else is awake and warn them.'

They could Jack Stroke now speaking with Eva. He too turned back to his room.

It was after ten o'clock before breakfast was announced and residents were summoned from their room by the day staff. There was a police officer outside the staff room and a blue and while ribbon cordoning that area off.

The residents were all round-eyed and nervous at all this unusual commotion. They went in and were served breakfast. Most of them were starving now and eagerly attacked their food. They had looked around at the tables and could see that all were present. 'So, what was the fuss about', they whispered under their breath?

It was after breakfast when Miss Swift came into the dining room. She was pale and her hair did not look quite as perfect as usual. She asked if they would all please gather in the lounge now, and Mrs. Wilson would make an announcement. Medication would be delivered to their rooms this morning.

They all looked at each other as they rose to their feet. Vera walked beside Jack Stroke and they pondered the mystery.

'It must be serious Vera if the police are here and the ambulance left earlier, Maggie saw it. We couldn't from our wing.'

Vera nodded. 'Can't imagine what it is, can you?'

On reaching the lounge and finding their usual seats, Mrs. Wilson entered and stood facing them.

'My friends, I hate telling you bad news but unfortunately I must. One of our regular night staff,

Mano found a dreadful scene on coming back from duty at the sick bay in the old house. His colleague Sid Walker had been attacked and was in the staff room.' Mrs. Wilson stopped here to dab her eyes with a tissue. 'He immediately called the ambulance, and I was alerted too. The police are here and will have to make enquiries to try and find out what happened. They will talk to you shortly and if anyone can shed any light on this terrible matter, please don't hesitate to speak to them or to me, if you prefer.'

'Is Sid dead?' whispered Maggie.

'No, he is unconscious but suffered a bad head injury'.

'Could it be that he fell?' Jack Other asked this.

'We don't know for certain what happened, but the police believe he was attacked. The staff window was open and normally at this time of year, it is kept locked.'

Mrs. Wilson left a room full of shocked people.
They gradually began speaking softly and each tried to remember if they heard anything at all during the night.

Jack Stroke commented that the coast was clear when he went into the office to restart the CCTV tape and he had not checked the staff room.

Vera said in a shocked tone, 'He could have been attacked while we were having our dance. How awful!'

Nobody said anything after this and returned to their rooms for the medicine which was going to be delivered there.

That afternoon, after the siesta, the police were again present and gathered the residents in the lounge.

They were interested in anything strange that they may have heard during the night. Everyone shook their heads. There was not much to be gleaned from these old people, the policer officer thought.

'If anyone knows anything at all, no matter how little, please let Mrs. Wilson know and it will be passed on. Any information about the injured man also, all will be considered confidential and no need for anyone to worry. At this moment, we are considering a break in, as the window was open in the staff room and the night was cold, so that is suspicious.'

Sylvie as usual, voiced everyone's question in her booming voice. 'What exactly were his injuries, officer. Was he stabbed or what?'

'No, madam, he has suffered a catastrophic head injury and is unconscious, in fact he may never regain consciousness again.'

This silenced them. When the officer left, they chatted among themselves about it.

'Sneaky as he was, I would not wish this on the poor devil.' Jack Other intoned this, and everyone nodded in agreement.

The rest of the day most of the residents kept to their room. Many of them slept, they were still very tired after the party and dance.

That evening, when all were refreshed after a long siesta, the lounge was humming with conversation and opinions. The air was full of suppositions and bits of conversation heard in passing the office or police officers.

'I heard that Mano had to be sedated, he was so shocked…..'

'The room was covered in blood and Sid was thought to have fought for his life….'

Each new revelation shocked the residents, and some were visibly nervous.

At nine o'clock, Mrs. Wilson arrived at the lounge. She knew her 'family' would need reassurance and comfort.

She told them that the incident could not have happened if the front door had not been left unalarmed. Sid should have alarmed the door when Mano left to help at the big house. The window could not have been opened without the alarm going off if the main door had been reset. Sid must have been busy and forgotten to do that. On his return, Mano had not had to put in the security code. The poor man was of course absolutely shocked and felt guilty as it was Mano who volunteered to go over to the sick bay.

Jack Stroke looked at Jack Other when this was said. He knew that it would be Sid who insisted that Mano go. The sick bay was no place for slackers and would mean non-stop work all night. Jack Other nodded at him and winked his eye. Nobody could remember Sid ever doing a session in the sick bay.

Mrs. Wilson was speaking of security and trying to allay the fears of the residents.

'The police are working on the theory that someone from outside broke in, for whatever reason, and that Sid surprised them.

At this, Sylvie stood up. 'Why on earth can we not have locks on our bedroom doors, Mrs. Wilson? I think we would all feel a lot safer if we could lock our doors at night, like we did at home.' She looked around at the others and most of those hearing, nodded their heads vigorously.

Mrs. Wilson coughed and said apologetically, 'indeed, I know how you feel. It is a matter of being able to reach anyone sick or unable to call for help that this procedure is common in all retirement homes.'

'But we have our panic button, Mrs. Wilson,' persisted Sylvie.

'Sometimes people would not remember that Sylvie, or perhaps not be able to reach it. We must consider those who are frail and helpless once they are in bed.'

Sylvie sat down, not at all pleased. Ivy beside her, put her hand on her arm in sympathy.

There was more news. Mrs. Wilson herself had opposed this, but the police were insistent. Every resident of the home must be spoken to by them.

Chapter 28

There was an air of excitement when Detective Inspector Savage arrived with his assistant sergeant. Most of the residents had never experienced this sort of thing before and all of them felt a morbid fascination about the whole incident. Nobody had been evenly remotely sympathetic about the poor victim. They had all experienced Sid's malicious and often sadistic tendencies. Some of the oldies, suffering from dementia in its many forms were quite detached from the whole thing.

The lounge was considered the best place to conduct the interviews as it provided a comfortable and familiar place for the residents. The television room would accommodate the residents waiting to be spoken to, and they would have an interesting DVD put on, to keep them entertained. Mrs. Wilson insisted that she be present to keep her 'family' from being upset or stressed. She told Detective Savage that he must be gentle, at all times, and if she felt any pressure being exerted on her people, she would call a halt to the proceedings.

The detective himself was widely experienced in all police work and had worked on many cases. To be sure, this was his first case involving a retirement home and he thought it a bit of a waste of time and his expertise. Who in their right mind would consider any of these old folk capable of murder?

His boss, the Chief Superintendent himself, Charles Meagher, had requested that Savage conduct the investigation, as, unknown to Aidan Savage, this was because he had an interest in Rosebank House. His late mother-in-law had been a resident and he knew it was a superior kind of home. He also knew Eva personally and was impressed with the woman. He felt drawn to her too in a more personal way. He spent some hours wondering how he could approach her and ask her to dinner. He was a widower and only in his late fifties. Maybe this case could bring them closer.

The young sergeant who accompanied the detective hoped he would learn a lot. He admired Savage and made meticulous notes of every word that Savage uttered.

'Right, we will start with the residents on the A wing, I think.

Mrs. Wilson nodded and immediately handed him a list of names of the people on that side. She first had to bring them to view the wing and explained that it overlooked the gardens. He insisted on seeing each room and noted the names of the residents and their rooms against the list in his hand.

By the time the interviews started it was noon and they would work until dinner time at one. Then the ones who had been interviewed could have their siesta.

Mrs. Wilson immediately saw that there could be a problem. She explained that most of the old ones needed their nap after dinner and asked that they might be interviewed first and the more mentally competent ones, after dinner.

Detective Savage saw that he was dealing with an intelligent woman who really cared for those in her charge and acceded to her request. There was then a bit of shuffling of names. It would not be possible to do one wing at a time.

Eva offered to put names in the order that she thought was appropriate and the detective had no choice but to agree.

The more competent people were approached and told not to report to the lounge until after dinner was over. Mrs. Wilson herded the others into the television room.

Sylvie, Vera and Ivy decided to take a turn around the gardens. They were still in shock and Sylvie still insistent that they should be allowed locks on their doors. Ivy agreed wholeheartedly with her friend.

Vera, thinking of her whiskey having been stolen agreed that they had a right to privacy.

On their return around the lake area, they met the two Jacks and Bob Grunt approaching them. Jack Other was pushing the wheelchair, although, as it was battery operated, Bob was able to propel himself. They passed the three women and paused for a word.

'Are you all prepared for the inquisition, ladies?'

They laughed and made to move off. Jack stopped them and admitted that he was worried. They all looked at him.

'What about our daring escapade on Friday night? Do you think we should confess first and all that?'

Vera had not thought of that. Neither had the others.

'Well, we don't know when Sid was attacked, do we? Maybe we should keep quiet unless it becomes obvious that they know we were not in our rooms for part of the night?' Jack pondered this aloud.

Sylvie nodded, 'for all we know, he might have been attacked while we danced. We didn't hear anything did we?'

They all shook their heads. It had been just two o'clock when they had finished and there had been no sound or sight of Sid. Of course, he could well have been asleep if he had taken the coffee that Jack had prepared beforehand.

Suddenly, their plight seemed damning to them. If they had drugged the poor man and then he was attacked, they could be held responsible, couldn't they?

Vera tried to ease their minds. 'If he were asleep, surely there would have been no need to attack him?'

'That's right. If he were asleep the burglar could have just come and taken whatever he wanted.' Bob

Grunt wanted a simple solution and was not looking forward to meeting with the detective.

Jack Stroke suddenly put his hand into his pocket. He pulled out a small plastic bag which clearly contained three tablets.

'What do you know, folk? I forgot to doctor the coffee! I must be losing it. How could I forget that?'

Relief now flooded all the faces.

Sylvie sighed, 'well, thank goodness you did, otherwise we would have all felt guilty.'

Jack laughed nervously. 'Yes, and there was that time I forgot to turn the CCTV back to its proper position, remember? I seriously think my memory is going. Does anyone else have this trouble?'

'*That* is why we are here Jack, isn't it? We are changing into useless old duffers, that's what.' Bob Grunt frowned and turned his chair around. 'I'm going back now, I've had enough.'

They watched as he wheeled himself back to the house. The ladies continued to walk back to the house now.

'Do you know, I am absolutely starving,' said Ivy. 'Who would have thought that one could eat at a time like this?'

'Well we should all have a good dinner; heaven knows how long we will be in there answering questions.' Sylvie tossed her head defiantly. 'I for one am not going to volunteer information. I will answer their questions but am not volunteering anything. If they find out about our dances, that will all be stopped, believe me, then what will life be like?

Detective Savage and his assistant were beginning to feel as if they were in an unreal world. The interviews were boring and not going anywhere really. Most of the residents did not know what they were being questioned about. One old dear thought she was being interviewed for a job.

'I have had lots of experience --I think,' she said in a clear voice. Then she lost confidence and looked over at Mrs. Wilson. 'I was excellent at my job in the post office, was I not, Mrs. Wilson?'

'Indeed, you were dear. But what these gentlemen want to know is, did you hear anything at all last night? You remember, it was Halloween.'

'What did I hear? Well the music of course and there was dancing, and it was all wonderful. I enjoyed myself and loved dressing up. You looked lovely Mrs. Wilson all dressed up as a witch.' She beamed at the two men sitting at the table.

'When you went to bed, do you remember hearing anything strange?'

The assistant was trying hard to concentrate, but his stomach was rumbling, and he thought lunch time would never come.

'Oh, I heard nothing in bed. I was so exhausted with the dancing I must have gone straight to sleep.'

And so, it continued. At one stage, Miss Swift put her head around the door to say that Sid's parents were on the phone. They were interviewing the second last one before lunch. Eva excused herself and left them.

The interview neared its end. The poor woman left them in sheer disbelief, and they were nearly laughing hysterically when they let her go. Then it was the last person in the television room to be interviewed

Detective Savage asked the man his name and asked how long he had been at the home. As it seemed he had only been there a short time, he was asked if he knew Sid Walker at all.

Duncan said he did not know the man, except to nod to. 'I have trouble hearing you know. These damn hearing aids are not all that they are cracked up to be, you know?'

The young assistant Tom Murphy tried to steer the conversation back. His belly could now be heard rumbling clearly.

'When did you last see Sid, can you remember Duncan?'

'Pardon me? Who is the lassie?'

Poor Tom tried to speak slower and pronounce his words more clearly. He felt that he sounded like a robot.

'Oh, I didn't see him at all. I try to steer clear of that one. Not a nice bloke at all, at all.'

Detective Savage wanted to know why that was?

'They call him Sid the Snake you know? Sneaky, that's what, and he gives poor old Rabbit grief, he surely does.'

'What time did you go to bed, can you remember, Duncan?'

'When everyone else went---when the dancing was over. Sure, I was drenched in sweat and had to sit in the shower for a while before going to bed. I tell you now, those women are something else.'

Chapter 29

Mrs. Wilson finished her sad phone call to the parents of Sid Walker. They were going to travel up that day to visit their son at the local hospital. They were shocked at the news. She felt for them and told them that they would be welcome to stay in her home while away from their own home. It took her some minutes before she could compose herself and return to the lounge to the policemen.

On entering the room, she was astounded to find the two men laughing their heads off, red in the face, and the younger of the two mopping his streaming eyes.

They sobered as soon as they saw Mrs. Wilson.

'Sorry Mrs. Wilson for appearing to be acting out of character, but that last man was so entertaining. Quite innocently too, I assure you. That and his deafness had us confused for a while.'

She told them that a good meal awaited them in the dining room, if they would like to avail of the service.

They left the lounge swiftly. They felt embarrassed at having been found laughing in the middle of such a serious investigation.

The food was delicious and plentiful. After their cup of coffee, the men felt a lot better.

The rest of the afternoon passed and the remaining residents who were interviewed were certainly more compos mentis. They were certainly shrewd enough and had to be prompted to remember, although Detective Savage felt that they all remembered clearly, the happenings of last night.

'No, I heard nothing once I went to bed. I usually fall asleep straight away, officer. Nothing disturbs my sleep, I assure you. Besides, it was a long day, and we were all entertained by the delightful children.' Sylvie gave her most girlish smile to the men.

They then veered off track and asked about Sid and why he was called Sid the Snake?

Sylvie was momentarily startled. How did they hear that, she wondered?

She laughed softly. 'Oh, that was a bit of a mistake I'm sure, he was a pleasant enough man. He just moved about softly and startled one, now and then when he crept up behind you. Not that he *crept* up, you understand, he just moved silently. So, I suppose the name came from that habit of his.'

They nodded and made notes. Detective Savage had a way of turning his head to the side but keeping his eye on you as he spoke, that made most people nervous. It was as if he suspected you of doing something that he knew about.

It worked now on Sylvie, who suddenly felt a hot flush coming upon her, and she had not had one of those for years. Now she knew her face was flaming red and perspiration broke out on her face and all over.

'I really do not know anything else that can help you officer and I really want to leave now if you don't mind.'

She rose in her chair and young Tom immediately got up and opened the door for her.

'Thank you very much Sylvie, you have been most helpful,' added Savage, although she had imparted nothing of interest. Her nervousness intrigued the men.

'I suppose you have to understand her unease. They live pretty uninteresting lives here; no excitement of any sort and suddenly, here we are, the guards, questioning the poor creatures,' Tom said thoughtfully.

They looked at their list and thought another hour should finish it.

Their next man was Mr. Burrow and immediately Detective Aidan Savage thought of a rabbit. His kids kept rabbits and this man reminded him of one. Then he remembered Duncan's story.

They gently asked the man his name and he told them it was Richard Burrow. He had not heard anything untoward the previous night and was shocked to hear about the attack. Did they think it was a burglary gone wrong, he asked? He leaned forward to hear their reply.

'At this time, we can make no assumptions, we just need to try and find out at what time the man was attacked and if anyone saw anything suspicious, either earlier in the evening or later that night.' Aidan Savage explained softly and slowly to the man. He felt the man was on tenterhooks and he looked quite frightened, rather like a poor little rabbit, he thought.

'It's really a dreadful thing to happen in such a beautiful place. I don't know how poor Mrs. Wilson will cope with this. She is so caring, you know.'

Both men felt that indeed this man was concerned for the owner of the home. He seemed sincere and gentle.

'Have you yourself had any dealings with this man Sid? Aidan Savage asked this with his head turned sideways and his eye on Mr. Burrow.

'Oh, no no! Goodness me, no!'

Straightaway Mr. Burrow was flustered and agitated. His colour changed and a tic appeared at the side of his mouth.

'Was he a pleasant person, would you say?' Tom Murphy played with his pen as he asked this, and Mr. Burrow's eyes immediately stayed glued to the pen.

'He was a decent enough human being, and he did not deserve to be attacked. Will he survive, do you think?'

They assured the man that Sid was in the best hands and would have the best care and he must not worry.

'Suppose the attacker should come back, though. Could it be that a psychopath is out there roaming around?'

When he was gone, young noted Murphy that Mr. Burrow made no complaint against Sid Walker.

'Surely if Sid had done anything to annoy him, he would have mentioned it?'

Aidan Savage leaned back in his chair and closed his eyes. He often did this when thinking.

'No, I think not, young Murphy Then he would have had to explain why he was targeted by Sid. He would rather that we didn't know anything about it, I think.'

Young Murphy wrote rapidly in his notebook then sat chewing the end of his pen.

The rest of the residents came and gave their reports, but nobody could remember hearing anything out of the ordinary last night.

'When was the last time you saw Sid?' asked Aidan Savage.

Jack Stroke sat in front of him, a tall lean man, with obvious weakness on his right side.

Jack thought. 'I think it was just before the children made their entrance. I was coming from the toilets and I noticed him standing outside the recreation door, which was open. He had his hand to his mouth and looked as though someone had kicked him in the stomach.' He looked at the men. 'That is exactly what I thought.'

'What was going on then, before the kids came?'

'We were just having our own party, a bit of a singsong, you know. We had a few games before that, nothing strenuous, but fun for us oldies.'

'You don't know if Sid was nasty to anyone in the house, do you, Jack?'

Aidan gave Jack his sideways look and saw Jack swallow and look away.

'He could be an aggressive bugger at times, but sure, can't we all?' He laughed lightly.

'Did you ever see or hear him being nasty to anyone?'

Jack looked as though he was thinking hard, then shrugged his shoulders.

'We all get on each other's wick now and again. It's only natural, you know.'

Aidan sighed. 'Yes, I understand that. If you all were smiling at each other all the time, it would surely be unnatural.'

Jack Other and the remaining women did not add anything of any importance to the general questions asked. Vera was a piano player who ran singsongs a couple of times a week; Maggie was the sort of woman you had for a mother-in-law-- if you were lucky; big and jolly and good natured; Ivy was like a little girl in an old body, smiling and eager to help, but also looking for acceptance and needy. Clingy, Aidan would think later. Nobody had a bad word to say about Sid, which was surprising as the newest resident had already dropped that brick. Still, maybe it was all in Duncan's imagination?

Aidan had to remind young Murphy that they were present at an old age home for a reason and not to take everything at face value.

'After all, can you imagine anyone of these people attacking a young strong man? The men don't strike me as being that assured. All these younger men go to gyms now and are into bodybuilding and that sort of thing. As for women, well, it's well known that women who murder, usually use poison.'

Young Murphy nodded and wrote furiously in his notebook. Thinking of poison, he prayed that his boss, who was so good to him would not ask him home for a meal. He would not be able to refuse, although it would take days for his stomach to recover from Mrs. Savage's exotic cooking.

As he drove home, Aidan went over the interviews in his mind. The thing that struck him was that nobody except Mr. Burrow had asked if Sid would survive.

He felt that there were some of the old people who knew more about Sid than they mentioned to him. It might be worth delving further in a week or so when people were more relaxed and hopefully Sid Walker had recovered or at least improved.

He stopped off at the hospital on his way home from his office to see if Sid were conscious. It would be very convenient if he were awake and able to give them his story.

Unfortunately, the news was not good. The neurosurgeon told him that Sid had suffered a catastrophic head injury and if he survived, would most likely be in a vegetative state for the rest of his life.

Chapter 30

Life was subdued in the house in the weeks following Sid's attack, but by mid-November, talk centred on the approaching Christmas and suddenly life got a little happier.

The carol practice was going well, and Mrs. Wilson was relieved to see all the residents getting back to normal. Jack Stroke had firmly rejected the idea of having the dance evenings for a while. There were two new people on now, four nights a week and Mano and another fellow Mauritian at the weekends. Everybody felt sorry for Mano, who had been questioned a lot by the police and detective. It was now known that Mano and Sid played a lot of cards here on their nights on duty and that threw some suspicion on Mano, who was owed money by Sid. Eventually however, they believed in the man's innocence, and besides, he had been working visibly all night in the sick bay.

There had been a spate of burglaries in the nearby town and suburbs recently that was keeping the police busy. They believed it was an organised criminal gang at work and they were involved with other forces from different counties. It was also questioned whether these criminals could have been involved in the break in at Rosebank and the attack on Sid Walker.

There was now an outbreak of Novovirus or winter vomiting at the retirement home and some of the residents were very ill indeed. Sylvie was one who was affected badly and had been moved to the sick bay in the old house.

Ivy was distraught and was not allowed to visit her as it is so highly contagious. Everyone tried to comfort the little woman and tell her that Sylvie would be fine, she was a fit woman. Ivy went round the place like a lost soul for the ten days that Sylvie was away. Maggie also had it and Bob Grunt, but they recovered well and soon things were back to normal.

There was now a craft class every Friday evening and everyone found something they were interested in. Vera and Sylvie loved making greeting cards and intended to send them to their loved one for Christmas. Knitting was popular too and everyone smiled when they found Rabbit Burrow knitting a hot water bottle cover. He was delighted with himself and smiled a lot these days.

Mrs. Wilson attended one of the afternoon singsongs coming up to December and was both surprised and impressed by the choir, which had now been joined by a few of the daytime staff. It gave her an idea.

Later that week she made a phone call to her new friend, the Mayor and told him her idea and asked what he thought of it. He was supportive of it and thought it a great way to put their town and its services on the map.

Vera was told later that day, that their concert was going to be televised by the national television channel and that the audience would include the Mayor and other dignitaries as well as the local schools and local services.

Vera was immediately nervous. 'I don't think we are ready or really good enough for that, Mrs. Wilson.'

'Now don't you worry. There will be other musicians joining you to give a bit more body. There is a musical group here in the town who have expressed great interest in this. You would be the musical director and they would play just what you want and have already practiced. There could be a few other solo performers if time allows. It would be such a good advertisement for Rosebank, don't you think?'

'Yes, I must say it sounds thrilling and I hope we are up to it. We might try and get more practice in, but of course we don't want them to worry about it too much.' Vera was nervous and hoped it would not show or else the whole bunch of them would be nervous.

Mrs. Wilson was please by Vera's response. 'I think it will be just the thing to get them all back on track. The attack on Sid set us all back a lot, we feel.

This will lift up their spirits and I feel it will be a great Christmas.'

'When should we tell them, do you think, Mrs. Wilson?'

'As soon as you like, Vera. Let them absorb the idea for a while, then when the other people join in for practice, they will not feel so strange.'

At the next singsong, Vera mentioned it to the choir. They were quiet for a few moments. Then the questions started, and the excitement began to affect them all.

'Imagine! We will be on the telly, our families will see us.'

They were all thrilled and put everything they had into the following practices.

The other musicians joined them the first week in December and after the first nervous beginning, spirits soared, and the excitement was palpable.

Mrs. Wilson was present at these practices. Her job was to time the entire performance and make sure they did not overrun their allotted time on television.

After the first two rehearsals, she found they had plenty of time over. She spoke with the musicians and Vera.

They discussed how they could draw out the carols to use up the time. Then Vera had an idea.

'What about a solo or better, a duet with backing by the piano and violins?'

Mrs. Wilson smiled broadly. 'I would love that Vera, and I feel that you already know who the two will be?'

'Yes, I do. Ivy has a most beautiful voice and Jack's voice would go so well with it. I'm thinking of "Mary's Boy Child", the verses sung by Ivy and Jack and the choir joining in for the refrain. How does that sound?'

Eva Wilson clapped her hands. 'That is a favourite of mine! I think that would use up the time we have. Let's try it.'

Maggie rummaged around for the carol in her briefcase and one of the staff photocopied out sheets for everyone.

Jack Stroke was a natural harmoniser. Ivy knew the carol as did they all. Ivy started on the first verse and Jack tried his hand at harmonising. Vera stopped playing and told him not to worry. They would work on the harmony until he had it off. They took off again and this time the instruments joined in softly with Ivy and louder when the choir came in for the refrain.

Mrs. Wilson and Vera were satisfied with the evenings work. The next practice was the last one before the live broadcast and would be timed by Eva again.

Ivy was in seventh heaven of course. She was gifted, but nobody had ever paid attention to her voice before. It was intoxicating. Sylvie was delighted for her and proud as well.

There was now choir practice each afternoon, with Jack and Ivy getting an extra thirty minutes afterwards to work on the harmony, for which Jack was well able

The night finally arrived. The residents had been getting ready since before supper. Everyone was dressed in their best and looked marvellous. Most of the ladies had their hair done that morning. Spirits were high and although nervous, they were quietly confident. The only one to pull out of the show, was Duncan, who did not have much of a voice anyway but was also terrified that his hearing aids would start 'shouting', as he called it.

The Mayor arrived and his entourage, the school children and teachers, some of the nurses from the local hospital and a doctor or two. All in all, the recreation room was nearly full, and chairs had been borrowed from the school to accommodate all. Detective Savage was also present, representing the police force and to his surprise, the boss had come too, the Chief Superintendent.

At eight o'clock sharp, the lights dimmed and all the television people, who had been there all afternoon, were now in charge. Mrs. Wilson gave a brief speech, welcoming everyone to Rosebank House and hoped that they would all enjoy the evening and the families watching at home also.

Vera wiped her hands once again. She felt so nervous. She knew that she would not be on view as much as the choir and that helped her control her nerves.

The outside musicians were all in place and the concert began. After the first carol had ended and the applause began, everyone relaxed and smiled at each other and the audience. They knew now that all would go well.

Mrs. Wilson was glancing now and again at her watch. She had allowed time for applause but hoped she had allowed enough time. The producer had told her not to worry, they could just run the credits and all that while the music faded gradually.

After three carols, to allow the choir some rest, the musicians played some Christmas music, just the four of them.

Finally, the end was there, and Ivy and Jack stepped forward to begin. Vera played the introduction with the violins and the duet began. The light was now just focused on the two, the rest of the stage setting was dimmed. The voices blended seamlessly, and the effect was magical. Not a sound was heard. The choir then joined in the refrain and the violins played a bit louder. Jack's voice was strong but did not drown out Ivy. His harmony was perfect.

It was so lovely, Mrs. Wilson thought, her eyes brimming with tears. Jack had Ivy's hand in his, he so tall and Ivy so small. There was something other-worldly about the performance.

The applause at the end was like thunder and it seemed to go on and on, forever. Even the Chief Superintendent was on his feet clapping like mad.

Then the lights came on in the recreation room and the television crew started unplugging all their equipment. The producer stepped up to the make-shift stage and congratulated all the choir and players.

He himself would soon be talking about the performance at the old age home. He thought if old people could perform like that, then maybe, old age was not that bad.

There were refreshments provided for all in the dining room. Later, when most of the audience had gone home, the Chief Superintendent was still there chatting to Mrs. Wilson and the staff. They spoke about his late mother-in-law who had outlived her daughter, his late wife. Miss Swift took this opportunity to ask about the investigation into the attack on Sid Walker.

'I have to say that we are not getting anywhere fast. We have been totally occupied of course, with the spate of local burglaries, but we will be renewing our efforts very shortly, I can assure you. I do not think that those burglaries were connected, with your break in here.'

Mrs. Wilson assured him that everyone here would help in whichever way they could and that the guards could call at any time to discuss anything they felt was relevant. The staff gradually slipped away.

The Chief Superintendent turned to Eva, as he walked towards the front door. 'Actually, I need to speak to you Eva. Can you call into the station when it suits you, although I think the sooner the better, if you can manage to?'

Eva Wilson was surprised but agreed readily. She could not imagine what the great Charles Meagher could want to discuss with her.

Chapter 31

The residents slowly returned to normality. Singsongs were the usual rowdy events although they did still practice their carols for the house party on Christmas Day. They were all looking forward to seeing themselves on television when the program would be relayed on national television a week before Christmas.

Eva visited Charles Meagher two days after the televised concert. For some reason she felt a bit nervous going into the station and asked to see the Superintendent. She told herself not to be so silly as she ascended the stairs to his office.

She need not have been worried. Charles was charming and thanked her profusely for being so prompt. As he spoke about his ideas, she became alarmed. He wanted to investigate more into the residents of Rosebank. She could hardly believe what she was hearing.

'But why, Charles? Do you for one minute, think that anyone of the family could have attacked Sid?'

'Eva, have you forgotten the quite unexplained and unexpected death of Ken Smith some months ago?'

'But that was not an attack. Surely that was an accident albeit an unusual one?' She looked at him askance.

'Eva, the forensic pathologist was not at all satisfied about the way the man died, hence all the examinations of Ken's room, do you remember? In fact, as soon as I told him about the latest attack, he became very curious about the injury that Sid suffered. He said it was a similar injury, crushing the brain and he would like to be kept informed of any developments.'

Poor Eva was bewildered. What was he proposing she asked?

'I have already spoken to my detective Aidan Savage and he agrees that he suspects that the residents, or some of them, at any rate, know more about Sid's attack than they are letting on. He proposed a plan of action and I have given my approval. Aidan thinks he would like to try a softer approach, he does not wish to alarm the old folk. He thinks his young sergeant Tom Murphy would be the one to do a bit of digging.'

Eva could only wonder whether the two men were serious and hoped that her incredulity did not appear on her face. She told the Chief that if he thought *that* would help solve the crime, then by all means send in the young man. She would not stand in their way and would encourage the residents to chat informally with the officer.

'Thank you, Eva, you do a wonderful job at Rosebank and with the ill people being treated in the old house, I know you are much appreciated in the town. I trust you will always feel that you can come and chat with me anytime, day or night.'

They shook hands and Eva departed, still perplexed.

Tom Murphy appeared the next day. He was not in uniform but casually dressed, with the approval and permission of the force's bosses.

The residents were merely told that Tom was there to chat with anyone who felt like a chat or if they were worried about security in the house. Sid was not mentioned.

The weather was dry and mild for December, so the residents were often found outside walking slowly, singly or in pairs.

Tom would simply wander around, now and then stop for a chat or sometime sit down on a bench beside a resident and initiate a conversation. People liked to talk and there were fewer visitors since the Novovirus illness. Relatives were being considerate and restricted in their visiting.

He spent part of each morning like this and then went back to the office and typed up his meetings with the various people he had chatted to. On a particular day he could hardly type, he was laughing so much. Really, he thought the place would provide a great series for television, the comedy was mighty.

In the coming days before Christmas week he spoke to Vera. He sat down beside her.

Vera immediately recognised him as the policeman. They chatted and he discovered that his mother was nursing with her daughter Judy.

'It is surely a small world,' she joked.

His mother was older than Judy and was very fond of her. She had often spoken of the nurses on her ward and Judy's name came up often.

Vera became silent for so long that Tom asked her if she was alright.

Vera shook her head and to her embarrassment started to cry. The story of Tommy came tumbling out and Vera's fears after hearing about his reputation. She knew in her heart that the boys were not happy and feared something would happen to Judy. After all, he already had a prison record.

Tom listened patiently and told the sad woman that he would make discreet inquiries.

'I'll make sure that we keep an eye on Judy, Vera. Try not to worry. If he once comes to our attention, we'll come down on him, like a ton of bricks. Could you let your daughter know that she must report any abuse if it occurs?'

Vera nodded sadly.

Then he turned the conversation around to the residents. Was Vera happy here? Were the staff kind to them all? Sometimes one heard of old people being abused in these retirement homes and it was a worry that some of them would be unable to complain.

Vera hastened to tell him that it was a most wonderful place, the staff were respectful and all lovely.

'All of them, staff and residents?' he asked.

'Well since old Ken went, life is easier, I think.'

Then the conversation continued with Vera explaining why Ken was called The Lech. He smiled when he heard the nicknames.

It was so easy to chat to Tom. He was a listener and most sympathetic. He felt so sorry for them, he confided to Vera; it must be a very dull life for able-bodied people like her and some others; no excitement or normality.

Vera laughed heartily and said not at all. Life was exciting in more ways than one. That had to be explained of course. She forgot completely that she was chatting to a police officer. She laughingly told him about their midnight escapades and how alive it made them all feel. Then she remembered the secrecy involved and warned him not to say anything to the authorities.

'The trouble with a lot of people,' Vera explained, 'is that they misunderstand old age and treat elderly folk like children most of the time.'

Then it was time for dinner and Vera thanked the man for listening and hoped to talk to him again sometime.

After lunch he met the little old lady, who had made he and Aidan laugh so much in their first interview. She was about to go off for a siesta but opted for a conversation instead.

This time he listened more carefully. She was still a bit scatty, flitting from one thing to another like a demented butterfly, still, he was gathering information. When he asked about the sore toe she had previously complained about, she beamed and said it was fine again. The toenail was regrowing and there was no soreness.

Her previous story to them about losing a toenail due to doing the tango had them in convulsions, but now he understood the story. It was not a story, it was true. He wondered how many other daft things they had heard and dismissed. He asked her a few more questions about her previously hilarious stories and made a mental note to ask more questions on the same subject to others. When the poor woman started yawning, he felt guilty and suggested that it might be time for her nap, she agreed readily and trotted off.

He decided he had done enough for the day and went back to his office.

The next day he got talking to the two Jacks who were out walking together. They were an amiable couple of men, Tom thought, but he still felt a bit of reticence on Jack Stroke's side. Jack O'Hara, or Jack Other as he was called was more forthcoming. He asked them innocent questions about the daily routine and whether the men found it boring.

The two Jacks wondered if the young fellow knew the meaning of old age. Did he expect them to be gadding about playing football or spending nights in the pubs?

'I've had a stroke, young Tom,' explained Jack 'and my friend here, another Jack, has Parkinson's and a tendency to forget his name now and again. That's why we are here and getting very well looked after, I may add. We have nothing to complain about. When you're in your seventies you don't need much to make you content.'

Jack Other agreed. 'We have everything we want and need. Eva Wilson is a great woman.'

Tom decided to go off piste for a bit. 'What about the fellow who died suddenly, a few months ago? Was he a happy chappy?'

Jack Stroke was silent, but the other Jack laughed.

'Ken was Ken and a bit of a lad. Liked the ladies a bit too much and it was not appreciated here. He had a bit of a past and all.'

'Oh! Famous, was he?' asked Tom.

'Not really,' said Jack Stroke, 'he played in a well-known local band here, years ago.'

'Until he ran away with the drummer's wife,' added Jack Other.

Jack Stroke shot him a look that was noticed by Tom.

There was not an awful more to be learned from them, Tom decided. Before he left them, he asked about the Halloween party and what they had dressed up as. If they were surprised by the question, they did not let on. Jack Stroke was dressed as Long John Silver, complete with eye patch; Jack Other had dressed as a clown.

Tom went back to the office in a thoughtful frame of mind. He did not even notice the blonde officer, Carol Moran hovering near his desk.

Chapter 32

The parents of Sid Walker were summoned on Christmas week. Their son had become conscious for some days now but seemed to have the mental capacity of a three-year-old child. However, after seeing the concert on the television in his old workplace, he had got visibly agitated. He had mouthed some unintelligible words and pointed his finger at the screen.

The staff had been delighted and thought this was a great step forward, even though the neurosurgeon did not believe he would regain his previous intelligence.

One dedicated young trainee nurse was sure she understood what he was trying to say.

'He is saying Mam mam, I'd swear to it.'

They decided to ask the parents to come anyway and see what would happen. They, poor things, expected to see their old son Sid, sitting up and welcoming them. What they did see, left them in no doubt that Sid was gone forever and that the surgeon was correct in his diagnosis. There was no recognition on the part of Sid. He was a dribbling baby again and the parents left in tears.

The young nurse was crushed too. She kept insisting that it was at the screen he was pointing. Someone got a recording of the show and put it on the DVD player when visiting was over. A few of the other nurses decided to watch and see if there was any reaction. The performance was repeated, and Sid was placed in a chair in front of the screen. He again showed signs of excitement and pointed his finger while articulating what some thought was jibberish, and some going closer thought it sounded like Maa'am, sounding rather like a sheep they thought.

The young trainee again was excited, and the ward sister agreed that he definitely recognised something or someone in the DVD. The fact that it had happened twice was enough to convince the sister and later the doctors, that Sid was not totally brain-dead.

More tests were ordered, and Mrs. Eva Wilson was also told about the so-called 'progress'.

She decided to give the good news to the residents after supper that night. She was also going to tell them more about Sid's background.

The residents were rather ambivalent about the news of Sid's recovery and just hoped he would not return to Rosebank.

Mrs. Wilson then told them Sid's story, which was rather sad. He had been taken into care at the age of three, his mother being deemed unable to care for him. She was in a mental hospital having been acquitted of murdering her husband, through lack of evidence. He was later adopted by a kind childless couple. He had had a difficult childhood and the

217

parents had tried counselling for him and seen all the paediatric psychiatrists available. The belief of the day had been that the child had witnessed his father's death, however it was caused, and that had damaged him. Finally, with the onset of puberty, he seemed to settle down and the parents had no more trouble with the lad. Sid had been a well -qualified nurse and had excellent references when he came to Rosebank.

There was silence after Mrs. Wilson finished the story. Everyone was now sorry that they had thought badly of Sid and called him a snake.

In the lounge the talk on Sid lingered.

'Poor child, what a pity we had no idea. We would have made a big effort to be nice to him,' Maggie moaned.

'Yes, childhood can have a lasting effect on a person,' Vera said. 'Maybe he will recover.'

'No, the doctors told Mrs. Wilson, there is no chance of that. He is like a three-year-old. That is ironic, isn't it, seeing as he was three when it happened.' Jack Stroke shook his head.

Jack Other said, 'maybe it would have been better if he had died.'

The next day Tom was back at Rosebank. The morning was colder. He went in to have coffee and see who was about to talk to. He could only see one person there, and approached the man sitting alone, looking out the window.

He went to introduce himself, but Bob Grunt muttered, 'I know who you are. Police.'

Tom knew that this was an uncooperative type of person. 'Indeed, I am, but I am not totally operating as a policeman. I just want to get an inside view of old age homes or retirement homes as they are called.'

'Really? Thinking of moving in?' Bob grunted.

Tom laughed easily. 'No, but my granny will soon need to move somewhere, I think. She's a danger to herself these days and doesn't want to move in with her daughter, my mother, who works anyway and could not easily look after her. I told Mum I'd suss this place out and see if it's all that it's cracked up to be. Have you been here a long time Bob?'

'Long enough. It's not bad as places go, I suppose. I would prefer to be in my own home, but as a double amputee, that's out of the question.'

Tom sympathised with the man. 'Was it diabetes?'

Bob nodded and grunted.

'I guess it must be pretty boring being stuck with all these oldies, especially if you have your faculties, as you appear to have.' Tom sipped his coffee and unwrapped a biscuit.

'No need to dismiss us all as oldies. We could show you young ones, a thing or two.'

'Well I would hate it, I think. I'm in a jazz band that we have started in the local force. We probably sound awful to the likes of you, but we think we're great.'

Bob turned and looked at Tom. 'Really, what do you play?'

'Oh, the only instrument I can play and the only one available as it happened was percussion; the drums.'

Bob chewed on this information. 'I played drums too, I was in the 'Wild Boys' in the late sixties and early seventies, way before your time.'

'Wow! Make any records?'

'Would have probably but the band broke up and that was that. We never got together again.'

'Shame. Still, you never lose the musical gift, do you? Pity you can't use it here and liven up the bloody place.'

For the first time, Bob Grunt chuckled. 'You'd be surprised by what we get up to here, boy. I get to play the drums.'

'Really, here? Does the staff go mad rock n' rolling?'

Bob looked around the empty dining room. 'We have some pretty hectic evenings, but it's strictly secret society stuff.' He tapped his nose and winked an eye at Tom.

'Maybe it would be the place for my Gran. She played the piano accordion in the past, maybe she could do it again. Is everyone musical, or just a few? What about the fellow that died, Ken?'

Immediately Bob Grunt's demeanor changed, and a scowl appeared. 'What made you bring that fellow's name up? He was a bad egg, and I am not sorry he gave his head a wallop off his locker. I'm out of here.

Chapter 33

Aidan Savage asked Tom Murphy how the inquiry was progressing, and the young man told his boss that he was making good progress. He sounded so confident that Aidan was inclined to be sceptical. He had a meeting with the Chief later and relayed the news.

'Let's get together with Tom later in the week and we'll see how things are going.'

Aidan agreed. 'I've been meeting with Social Welfare and digging back over the past forty years, investigating past lives.'

He was fatigued with all the searching through papers so old and yellow. He wondered why all this had not been computerised and was told that most of it had, nationwide. Theirs was such a small place that it had slipped through the net, somewhere. He felt he was nearing an important point in the investigation.

He would be glad to get shut of this investigation. It bothered him think of crime being committed in retirement home, a place which should be safe and secure for all the inmates.

Mrs. Wilson was also anxious for this case to be finished with. It felt as if something was hanging over Rosebank and her own home too. She encouraged all the residents and staff to help the young officer as much as possible so that he could depart and leave them all in peace again.

Tom was on the last round of informal 'chats'; he was anxious to see a couple of ladies that were never to be seen in his meanderings. That large lady Sylvie and her 'sidekick', as he thought of Ivy.

Today he struck gold. There was Ivy walking with Jack Stroke ahead. He lengthened his stride until he came alongside of them.

They greeted him civilly enough.

'Hi Long John Silver and how goes it with the pirate today?'

Jack grinned and shook his head. Tom Murphy turned to Ivy. 'And who, pray, were you dressed as? Bride of Dracula or Little Red Riding Hood?'

Ivy smiled at him mischievously and said, 'Not me, I was a leprechaun.'

If Tom looked startled, it was not noticed. 'Who then was the bride of Dracula? I've heard conflicting reports.'

'There was no bride of Dracula, Sylvie was the bride of Frankenstein and Vera was Mrs. Dracula.'

'Ah, that's why I was confused. Did anyone go as Dracula or Frankenstein? Was he Mr. Burrow?'

They both laughed at this. 'Poor Mr. Burrow, no, he went as the Lone Ranger,' said Ivy.

'Wasn't much of a costume, just a stetson and a pistol on his hip and knee-high boots, he borrowed from Annie.' Jack laughed as he told Tom this.

Jack then saw Vera and said he had to go and have a word with 'Fingers'.

'Is that what they call Vera? Oh, I get it, because she plays the piano, right?'

'Right.' Ivy replied.

'Where is your friend Sylvie today, do you know, Ivy? I must have a word with her before I finish at Rosebank.'

'Oh, are you not coming here anymore? We shall miss you.' Ivy sounded genuine.

'My granny will be needing a place soon, Ivy. Would you recommend it yourself?'

'Tom, it is a lovely place, home from home, only better. I've never been happier.'

'When did you come here Ivy? How did you hear of the place, you are not from around here, are you?'

Ivy hesitated a moment. 'No not from around here, a bit further away. Well I would not have known about it except for my friend Sylvie. When she moved here, she insisted that I come with her.'

'Really? Were you working with her?'

'Working for her, Tom. She rescued me from a terrible place. She pulled strings and talked to all kinds of people to get me out of there. I'll always be grateful to Sylvie, she is kindness personified, she....oh, there she is, coming towards us.'

Ivy waved wildly and shouted: 'we're over here Sylvie.'

They all met up and Sylvie looked surprised to see Tom. Then she glanced at Ivy's happy face and she looked suspiciously at Tom.

'What are you two up to then?' She asked.

'We were just telling Tom about the Halloween party and what we dressed up as,' Ivy explained to Sylvie. Then on seeing Sylvie's face, she added humbly, 'that's all, Sylvie.'

Tom forced himself to laugh loudly and shake his head. 'I'd love to have been there and seen Long John Silver with the eye patch. I'd say he looked the part.'

Sylvie visibly relaxed. 'We all looked great, but what would the police want to know that for?'

Ivy interrupted her. 'Sylvie, his granny may be coming here soon, and he wants to know what sort of a place it is.'

'Well I would recommend it highly, officer. Mrs. Wilson is a wonderful woman and I have known her a long time,' Sylvie boomed, while fixing Tom with a steely eye.

Tom looked earnestly at her. 'It does seem to be a lot better than I would have expected. Gran might take a bit of persuading though.'

'Most people do not want to end their life in a home that is not theirs, one just has to adjust. Isn't that right Ivy?'

'Absolutely, Sylvie.'

Tom thought he had better not seem to be over curious and said that he better be off and try to see Mrs. Wilson and mention his granny.

'Bye, Tom, it's been nice talking to you.' Ivy waved her hand.

Tom went to see Mrs. Wilson in her office. She offered Tom a cup of coffee, but he declined. He told her that he had made his round of interviewing the residents and would not be returning.

'There are just a couple of questions we need to know about the background of your people here.'

'What can you tell me about Sylvie's background. Is she a wealthy lady, would you say?'

'Yes, she came from a wealthy background but unfortunately they lost a lot of money due to risky investments. She managed to sell her house and that's when she arrived here. Her husband was a bank manager with various business interests. He died suddenly of a massive heart attack, which was awful for poor Sylvie. Her husband and mine knew each other and played golf at the local club although her husband Brian, was a good bit older.'

'So, you would have socialised with them a bit?' he asked.'

'No, not really, we were not in the same social circle. The golf was the only place where both men met occasionally.'

Tom nodded and then asked about Ivy. 'They seem very friendly. I'd say they have known each other for a long time. Am I right?'

'Absolutely right. Sylvie was a wonderful worker and got involved with many charities here. She used to run a hostel for unmarried mothers and later it was used as a refuge for abused women. She rescued many women for bad relationships and set up support groups for women coming out of prison and mental hospitals. She worked tirelessly for the less well-off.'

'What about Ivy? Was she by chance, one of Sylvie's protégées?'

'Well I do not know Ivy's background at all. She was working for Sylvie as a housekeeper. She was first brought in to help the aging housekeeper and when she died, Ivy took over and by all accounts, was hard working and extremely competent. She might come across as scatty sometimes but really, she is highly intelligent. It was poor Ivy who found Brian dead in bed, Sylvie was away that weekend. It must have been an awful shock to the poor woman. That, and having to telephone Sylvie with the terrible news.'

Tom stood up and thanked Mrs. Wilson profusely for her time and her understanding.

'We are sorry if we caused you any inconvenience Mrs. Wilson, but under the circumstances, we could leave no stone unturned to try and solve the crime.'

'Thank you, Tom but it was no inconvenience. Poor Sid suffered a horrible injury. His poor parents are distraught. They are decent people, and this is a dreadful blow to them.'

Tom left Rosebank House and did not expect to return there again. He now had to go and visit the parents of Sid and he was not looking forward to that.

As he exited through the front door, he nearly bumped into Vera. 'Well hello, Vera, or should I call you "Fingers"?'

Vera laughed. She had known she was called that for a while now and thought it could have been a worse name than that.

Tom lowered his voice and taking her arm, led her a few feet away from the door.

'I have mentioned that personal business you are worried about to my superior. The police station in the area they live in, have been quietly notified. If your daughter has any complaints tell her that Sergeant Marie Duffy is the one to ask for.

Vera was relieved that Tom had not forgotten the conversation and decided that she would ring Judy and give her that information. It would surely stay in her daughter's mind if things should unravel.

Later she rang Judy. In three days, it would be Christmas and she knew that her daughter would probably have to work part of the holiday. She was relieved that Judy answered the phone. She had a long chat with her and then the boys. Then it was back to Judy and Vera asked when she might be able to visit her. Judy was working over Christmas as Vera suspected, but as soon as duty ended, she was taking a week's holiday and would come with the boys to visit.

Vera was delighted. She could not bring herself to tell Judy the name of the woman at the police station. She would wait until she saw her. Judy told her that all her friends had watched the carol evening on the television.

She asked if her whiskey was running low and Vera said it was. There was no way that she could confess what happened to her whiskey twice. Judy would be annoyed and feel that she should complain.

Judy promised that she would ring on Christmas morning and hoped it would be a happy one for her.

Chapter 34

Tom was busy typing up his notes. He had been working nonstop, reviewing his written notes taken immediately after interviewing the residents of Rosebank.

He wanted to have all the facts at his fingertips when his boss called on him. He was so busy he failed to notice the lovely Carol as she passed and repassed his desk. The office party was coming soon, and she was hoping that Tom might show a bit of interest in her.

The call came as he came back from lunch, which had been a hasty sandwich from across the road.

He and his boss, Aidan Savage ascended the stairs together to the Chief's office. Aidan told the young Tom not to feel nervous, the Chief was a warm man and very encouraging.

Tom was taken aback. He was in no way nervous at all, in fact he was brimming with excitement. He had a lot to tell them.

The two men sat on the other side of the big desk. The Chief welcomed them and asked if they would like coffee. Tom said he would. He had not taken the time to have a cup with his sandwich. Savage also said yes.

Now the facts were due. Savage started by saying that he had ascertained the name of Sid's birth mother. It was Hilda Drew. She had been acquitted of her husband's murder although the police at the time were certain she was guilty. Through lack of evidence she got off but had to attend a mental hospital. The murder had taken place thirty-three years ago.

'What exactly happened the husband, how did he die, and where did he die?' The Chief wanted to know this.

'He was found at the bottom of the stairs at home with serious head injuries and died at the scene. Hilda always maintained he tripped and fell down the stairs. He sustained catastrophic head injuries. Her story never wavered.'

'Well, maybe she was innocent?'

Aidan hesitated, 'that was my first thought. However, records at the local hospital where her baby was born, showed that she had been admitted many times with suspect injuries; broken ribs, a dislocated jaw, in fact quite a few fractures over the years.'

'When she gave birth did these injuries cease? '

'No sir, they continued, but more seriously, the baby was admitted a few times with fractures. The social services were informed, but unfortunately, they were not as efficient as they are nowadays. Also, the family left the area and seemed to disappear off the radar, until the husband's death that is.'

'Sounds like she must have had an awful life.' The Chief Superintendent sighed and sipped his coffee.

'Thirty-three years later and domestic abuse still goes on. This is something that will always be with us, I fear.'

The Chief asked about the woman in the mental hospital. 'Don't tell me the poor creature is still there, Aidan?'

'Oh no. She was treated for a couple of years there and was then released. She did not get her child back; she was still considered unfit to be a mother. The trail goes cold after that.'

'Now young Tom, have you got anything important for us, from your time with the oldies?' The Chief turned his attention on the younger man.

Aidan also turned to his young assistant. *He* had delivered all his hard-won information and now wanted to hear Tom's findings.

'Well I can tell you that the residents at Rosebank have a rather more exciting life than would appear. They have a well-structured life, apparently. They all have the greatest respect for Mrs. Wilson, and they consider themselves fortunate to be in such a place.

I have interviewed them all in an informal way and compared the information I got, with the interviews that Detective Savage and I did, the day after the attack.'

He looked down at his notes and continued. 'I have picked up a few interesting items. Nobody had a bad word to say about Sid Walker, it seems. The only one to say something different was the person who has only recently joined the house, Duncan Power. He did not like Sid and made out that he was an unsavoury sort of man, hence the nickname I suppose, "Sid the Snake." He also mentioned that Sid had given Mr. Burrow a hard time, although nobody else mentioned that.

Most people disliked Ken Smith who was nicknamed "Ken the Lech". The ladies had nothing good to say about him. Then I discovered an interesting bit of information, given on impulse, I feel. Ken was a guitarist in a band call the Wild Boys, in which Bob Grant, nicknamed Bob Grunt, was the drummer. It seems that Bob's wife ran off with Ken the Lech. Naturally, Bob did not say anything about that.'

'How do you think their lives are exciting Tom?'

The Chief was now curious as was Aidan Savage.

'When we interviewed the day after the murder, we dismissed a few of the claims made by the inmates as daft and ridiculous. In fact, some of the oldies were hilarious.'

Detective Savage smiled and nodded his head.

'One old dear said she had lost a toenail from dancing the tango. She thought she was being interviewed by us for a job,' Aidan smiled at his boss.

All three men chortled at this.

'But it seems it was the truth,' continued Tom. 'They have 'naughty' evenings, usually on Fridays when they have illicit parties in the recreation room, starting at midnight and going on until two in the morning. They love these evenings and think it keeps them young.'

Savage interrupted, 'did they admit all this to you Tom?

'Not everyone spoke of it as it's considered a big secret and they are probably afraid they would not be allowed to continue, if it were known by the staff. The tango is a popular dance that they all partake in, don't ask me how, Sir; some can hardly walk without a stick or a frame.'

The men were still chuckling.

'Vera is the pianist and confided in me about the parties, also Bob Grunt, who plays the drums at these dances.'

'Oh, my word! Whatever will poor Eva say about this?'

'Must we tell her, Sir? Those oldies thrive on it.' Tom looked upset.

Savage asked if there was anything more.

'Yes, sir, do you remember how we laughed when old Duncan turned back as he was about to leave the room, after we had interviewed him?'

'Indeed, I do. When we asked if he slept well that night, he said yes, except for the security light outside waking him. The old lad swore he saw a leprechaun dancing across the lawn in the moonlight, heading toward the lake.' Savage laughed again.

'Well sir, this is interesting; there was a person dressed as a leprechaun that night, which Halloween. It was Ivy.' Tom closed his notebook.

Chapter 35

It was Christmas Eve and there was an air of suppressed excitement about the house. Susie and Annie were busy fixing presents around the base of the tree in the hall and other members of the staff were checking all the other rooms for decorations. The lounge also had a Christmas tree as did the recreation room and dining room. Mrs. Wilson flitted about checking everything and talking to the chef about the food and drink and checking that there would be no shortages in anything.

The residents were busy also, some were finishing their greeting cards in the recreation room and the artist Paul had dropped in to see them all. Ivy had done a lovely pastel for her friend Sylvie for Christmas and Paul was helping her put the finishing touches to it. She had bought a frame while in town last week, after church and he helped her to frame the picture.

Vera was tinkling on the piano and going over the order in which the carols would be sung tomorrow. There would be church of course and after that, presents would be distributed. Everyone would be offered a sherry before lunch and then after that, there would be a short siesta; the carols would begin then and there would be cakes and more wine for whoever drank. It would be a relaxed evening and hopefully very entertaining with staff contributing as well.

Vera planned to ring Judy immediately after dinner, as she thought it better if she rang her. Judy would not be eating dinner until five or six o'clock.

The last people the residents expected to see in the house, were the police. They had appeared as some of the residents were going to take their siesta.

Mrs. Wilson was seen bringing two police officers into the office. There were different men to the ones they had seen before.

Jack Other and Jack Stroke noticed them and looked at each other.

They guessed the CCTV tapes would be examined. It made sense did it not? Jack Stroke had been expecting this and wondered how it took them so long.

He decided it was time to make a clean breast of it to Mrs. Wilson. Better to do it before it was discovered, and God only knew what the police would make of it.

He waited until the woman emerged from the office.

'Wish me luck Jack, I'm giving myself up without a fight and I take all the responsibility.'

He approached Mrs. Wilson and asked for a quick word with her, it was important, he said. She led him down the hall to her own private small office and smiling at him, told him to sit down.

She was not smiling after Jack's confession and found it difficult to believe that all this happened. It was an old age home! How could they have behaved like precocious children. Was this due to dementia, she wondered? She had always felt that Jack Stokes was a sensible and coherent man, not at all vacant like some of them.

At the end of it all, Jack contritely apologised and took responsibility for the escapades.

'Jack, you do realise that this could have all ended tragically. Most are infirm and unsteady on their feet, including yourself. What would have happened if anyone fell and suffered a broken hip or leg. The legal implications are horrific. I am most surprised that Vera agreed to it.'

'Now you must blame nobody but me, Mrs. Wilson. The others were so in favour and have enjoyed it so much, and it was myself that arranged to fiddle with the CCTV.'

Mrs. Wilson sighed and leaned back in her chair. 'Well, we have all noticed an improvement in the residents for the past six months. I just wish you could have come and discussed it with me first.'

'Yes, we would all have liked to have done that, but knowing the answer, because of insurance and such like, decided we had to do it secretively. It actually added to the fun. We felt like children again.' Jack smiled wanly.

'Indeed, it seems like you have all entered your second childhood. It cannot continue after this, of course. We will have a discussion in the New Year and see if an afternoon of dancing can be arranged. We will need extra staff to help.' Mrs. Wilson rose to her feet and Jack got to his, knowing the interview was over. He smiled to himself as he returned to the lounge. An 'afternoon' of dancing; he thought of the wild antics of some of them; the tangos, the Hucklebuck and the rock and roll and he knew that if Mrs. Wilson, and the staff had seen that, they would not have believed their eyes.

Mrs. Wilson had another visitor that afternoon after the two officers were finished in the office scrutinising the CCTV tapes. Detective Inspector Savage called. He now knew that the tapes had been altered a few times over the past six months. Mrs. Wilson at once agreed with him and explained that Jack Stokes had been to see her and confessed to being guilty of fiddling with them to enable the residents to have an illicit evening's entertainment.

The detective was relieved that he did not have to break the news to the woman. She sounded remarkably calm about it all. However, there was more to his visit. As he sat in her office, and explained about the digging he had recently done, and the latest information he had just received. Her demeanour changed and she looked a trifle taken aback.

'Should I say anything, do you think?'

'No, not just now, I think. We need to sort out our own problems first, with an unexplained death and an attack. Now, I hope we can leave you in peace over the coming days and that you will all enjoy a peaceful Christmas and New Year.'

Chapter 36

Breakfast was well attended on Christmas morning. They were all up early and bright eyed for the most part. Some had to be reminded of what day it was of course, but the decorations and lighted Christmas tree in the dining room, had them all as excited as young children.

The staff and extra volunteers were here today. A large coach would take them all to church and almost all wanted to attend

At eleven o'clock Mrs. Wilson got a call to say that the big coach had broken down and they would have to send two other buses for the residents. That was awkward and would mean a couple more staff must attend if they could. The only available people were working in the sick bay and could not be left go. In the end, two volunteers from town agreed to meet the buses in town and accompany residents back to Rosebank house afterwards.

They all piled onto the buses, the wheelchair cases first, only two of them as one of the old ladies was suffering from a cold.

The talk on the buses was loud and cheerful. Susie and Annie were there and a couple of others.

After the religious celebrations in the two different churches, the residents were all herded towards the car park where the two buses were waiting.

Some of the oldies dozed off on the return journey some of the others started singing Christmas carols and discussing the pending dinner. Would it be turkey and ham or would there be a choice. Duncan hearing clearly, thought that there should be a choice. He did not like turkey and would prefer lamb. Maggie told him he was fortunate to have a nice hot dinner at all and to cop himself on. Much laughter ensued.

On reaching Rosebank everyone dispersed to their rooms to get ready for dinner. Outdoor shoes were put away and comfortable ones, or slippers were put on.

Sipping sherry in the lounge was a novelty. The two Jacks looked awkward holding the dainty glasses and muttered to each other that a stiff whiskey or brandy would be more to their liking. Mr. Burrow, overhearing them, admitted that he liked a sherry himself and hoped the wine would be good.

Sylvie sailed into the lounge like a cruise ship, as usual, and announced loudly that she would absolutely love a game of bridge later. Mr. Burrow smiled and told her that he would be delighted if they could play.

Vera was feeling tired and a bit out of sorts, though why, she could not explain. She looked around the room and wondered where Ivy was. She sipped her sherry and wondered if she could grab a second one. She intended to have a good sleep before the evening carols. When they had all been served sherry, Mrs. Wilson, Miss Swift and Susie and Annie came in with the hamper of Christmas presents. They all sat expectantly like children, smiling at each other.

They were all given presents carefully wrapped and a great deal of thought went into each gift, chosen by Eva and Susie.

The men were given gifts of after shave lotion, or socks, ties or slippers. Susie had been observing the needs of the residents all through November and presented the list to Eva. The women's gifts were more varied. Sylvie got a bottle of her favourite perfume as did Maggie and others, Vera got hand and face cream and there were lots of slippers and scarves and gloves given.

Eventually Eva, being handed the last of the presents, looked around and called, 'Ivy, where are you hiding?'

There was no reply and Eva looked anxiously around the room. Sylvie looked around also and then suggested that Ivy was probably in her room, would she go and get her?

Eva Wilson, recalling the detective's information, suddenly went pale and shook her head. She told Susie to run up and see if the woman was in her room. People were opening their gifts and some staff were moving about picking up the discarded Christmas paper.

Then dinner was announced, and all proceeded to the dining room where the fairy lights made the ordinary room almost magical. The residents were all ready for dinner now. Today there were name places set and Annie and Miss Swift helped them all to find their places.

Jack Stroke, walking beside Vera, asked if she had seen Ivy, had she been on her bus?

Vera paused. 'No Jack, I cannot say when I saw her last, but she may be in her room as Sylvie says. She walked along the table until she found her name. She looked at either side of her and found that Jack Stroke's name was beside hers. She called to him and pointed at the place next to hers.

She glanced at the opposite table and saw Sylvie looking expectantly at the door of the dining room. She was looking a bit worried or impatient, Vera could not tell which.

The room was buzzing with conversation and the clatter of cutlery soon put any thoughts of Ivy out of Vera's head. There was extra staff serving today and constant motion between the kitchen and dining room. Then they were pouring wine for whoever wanted it, a choice of red or white. Everyone accepted a glass and Duncan could be heard asking if there was not any rosé and muttering darkly when told there was not.

Jack was silent and watching the coming and going of all. He was the one who noticed that Mrs. Wilson and Susie were missing.

Eva Wilson was panic stricken when Susie came and said that she had searched all over for Ivy and could not find her.

The volunteers from the town were gone and nobody seemed to have seen Ivy after church.

After thirty minutes searching the grounds and house, she made the decision to ring the police station, then on second thoughts, she went to her desk and looked up the number for Aidan Savage.

She apologised to the man for interrupting his festivities and explained the problem of having a missing resident. The detective listened and told Eva that she did the right thing, and this needed careful handling. He told her that he was on his way.

He rang a couple of numbers before he left his house and had a good idea of where he would be heading with Eva. Mrs. Savage and children were not too happy to see work taking over even on this special day.

The detective also put another call through to his boss, Charles Meagher.

Chapter 37

As Mrs. Wilson waited nervously in the hall for Detective Inspector Savage to arrive, she fretted about how Christmas day was evolving and how it would end. She only ever wanted what was best for her 'family' as she called the residents. She had planned to bring the gentle Susie with her, but the detective had another idea. He put it to her that Sylvie appeared to be her confidante and felt that Ivy would be more at ease in her presence. Susie went and quietly summoned Sylvie from the dining room where all the residents were gleefully pulling crackers and nobody noticed Sylvie rising and going with Susie, except for the watchful Jack Stroke.

Tom Murphy drove, and Aidan Savage explained where they were going. The hospital where Sid had been treated, had only transferred the patient recently to the long-term care facility further north. There was nothing further that could be done for him at the hospital, and the rehabilitation centre available, might be able to provide some assistance, it was decided.

Sylvie, who had been very articulate in her protests at being brought like this, without proper notice, was now uncharacteristically silent.

Mrs. Wilson gently asked if she had any idea where her friend was going that morning after church? Sylvie tossed her head and replied, 'Of course not'.

This did not ring true to Aidan or Tom. There had been much discussion about the close relationship that was obvious to all. There was a mutual feeling that Ivy was somehow in thrall of Sylvie or under her influence unduly.

The miles passed soon enough, and each individual was absorbed in their own thoughts. Eventually, Tom turned off the motorway and they came to the entrance after a few miles of narrow twisting country roads.

As they got out of the car, the Matron appeared at the hall door of the once, stately house.

They spoke quietly in the hall and then Matron accompanied them along a corridor. Each door was open and the patients visible in their beds or sitting out in a type of reclining bed/chair.

It was as they got to the end of the corridor that Matron put her finger on her lips. Two nurses could be seen outside a room, one on either side of the doorway.

As they neared the room, they could hear the beautiful haunting melody so loved by Ivy. They crept closer, not wanting to disrupt the scene. Matron beckoned them into another room adjacent to the end room. There was a window between the rooms, and the patient and his visitor were easily recognised.

Ivy was sitting with her back to the viewers. She was leaning forward holding one of Sid's hands, with her other she was gently stroking his brow. The patient was gazing rapt into her face, his mouth open and dribbling saliva. He was sitting propped in a bed/chair.

The Matron whispered, 'she has been like this for hours, singing the same song over and over. We didn't know what to do; it is obvious that he recognises her, when she stops, he says something like Mam or Mama.'

Eve Wilson could not stop the tears which began to roll down her cheeks. She had to make an effort not to sob out loud. It was a heartbreaking scene. Even the men beside her appeared to be moved. Only Sylvie stood straight backed and did not appear to even see Ivy.

Ivy's beautiful voice continued, fluid, like water, the twisting, lilting, sad lament. Sid's eyes were beginning to close and Ivy began again.

'Where Lagan stream sings lullaby, there blows a lily fair, the twilight's gleam is in her eye, the night is on her hair'

Tom and Aidan made a move to leave but Eva stopped them, her hand on Aidan's arm.

'No please. Just let her finish and they you must go in.'

So they waited for the concluding words ot the Celtic air   'for Love is Lord of all…..'

This time, Sid's eyes remained closed and he slept.

Ivy stroked his face once more and then arose. She was so stiff after being in the same leaning position for so long. She could hardly straighten her back. Then she became aware of her onlookers. The frightened look disappeared as soon as she caught sight of Sylvie.

'He knows me, Sylvie, my William knows me.' She smiled at them all 'My baby still knows his mam.' She started to giggle manically.

The men came over and told her that they must go now and leave the patient to sleep. The woman nodded and said that sleep would cure him, that was all he needed.

Ivy was escorted out to the car with Sylvie on one side and Eva on the other. Tom started up the car and the detective sat beside him.

In the car, Ivy could not stop chattering. She alternated directing her face to Eva and then to Sylvie.

'You must not say too much Ivy, you have had a traumatic reunion. Best to stay quiet for now.' Sylvie tried her best to glare at Ivy, but the woman was too wound up to notice.

'No, I must speak about him. All these years I have wondered where he was and what he was like. To think that he was in the same place as me, I just cannot believe it.' She giggled hysterically for a few seconds, and then ran her hands through her hair.

'Oh, if I had only known it was William, I would not have hit him with the bottle. I don't know what stopped me hitting him again and again, like I did Ken. Something stopped me and I am so glad.'

Tom looked over at Savage and nearly hit a ditch. Mrs. Wilson looked at Ivy in disbelief. Sylvie looked out the window.

Ivy began to sing again happily, 'Where Lagan streams sing lullaby'…. She could not be stopped.

Ivy was admitted to the mental hospital three days later. There had been disbelief and shock for all the residents of Rosebank House. Sylvie was questioned a couple of times by the two members of the police force familiar to the residents.

There was no doubt that she knew Ivy's background thoroughly. She had fought hard for the patient in the mental hospital to be released and offered her a job. Ivy had been reassessed from time to time and was considered totally rehabilitated and normal again.

She would not tell Detective Savage why she took such an interest in Ivy. She had worked for many charities it was true and was generous with her time and money. Everyone who had known her, agreed with this. However, the detective could not wholly except that it was altruistic reasons only, that made

Sylvie 'adopt' Ivy. He suspected there was a darker reason, but too much time had elapsed now, to start digging into her own husband's death. Unless the woman herself confessed to influencing Ivy, they would all go on believing Brian had suffered a fatal heart attack. Perhaps, someday Ivy would be able to throw a light on what happened the man. Perhaps it was just a heart attack after all. Detective Savage intended to visit Ivy sometime later when she had settled into her new home. Little did the man know what the immediate future held in store for the world, and especially, for the residents of Rosebank House.

Printed in Great Britain
by Amazon